THE DEVIL'S DANCE

When Chris leaves New York for a vacation with her half-sister Pam, who is staying at a Tennessee country mansion, she discovers that the remote backwater is the site of a centuries-old feud raging between the Andrewses and the Melungeons; and Chris's elderly host, Mrs. Andrews, lives in fear. Danger lurks everywhere, from the deceptively tranquil countryside to the darkly handsome, yet mysterious, Gabe who hides amid the shadows. And when events take a more sinister turn, it seems that the curse of the Melungeons is hungry for more victims . . .

V. J. BANIS

THE DEVIL'S DANCE

Complete and Unabridged

LINFORD
Leicester

First published in Great Britain in 1979

First Linford Edition
published 2015

A catalogue record for this book is available
from the British Library.

ISBN 978–1–4448–2374–5

Published by
F. A. Thorpe (Publishing)
Anstey, Leicestershire

Set by Words & Graphics Ltd.
Anstey, Leicestershire
Printed and bound in Great Britain by
T. J. International Ltd., Padstow, Cornwall

This book is printed on acid-free paper

1

It was the Bozo that did it. And the Melungeons. Had it not been for that formidable pair, I would have gone to Florida for a month of warm sun and white beaches. There would perhaps have been a few mildly romantic memories of brief flirtations that, in the telling at the office, would take on a luster that had not been theirs at the time.

I traded those pallid and harmless memories for packs of wild dogs, for Big Betsy, the moonshine queen, for romance and mystery and terror. And all because my sister — half-sister, actually — signed her letter Bozo instead of Pam.

Since we were little girls that name had been a signal. We had taken early to attributing most unpleasantness to Bozo, the little stuffed clown: 'Pam, I think Bozo is afraid with the lights off,' or, 'Chris, Bozo thinks we'll get spanked if we do that.'

So, when her letter came signed Bozo rather than Pam, I knew it meant something — that she was unhappy, or afraid, or lonely — something contradictory to what she said: 'Everything is fine.'

Then there were the Melungeons: 'They're completely fascinating,' she wrote. 'The only authentically American monster myth that I know of. Devil worship and bloodshed and things that would make a good Christian's spine freeze. And I can hardly wait to tell you about Big Betsy, the she-devil moonshine queen.'

I read the letter, and reread it. I thought of Florida, the beaches waiting. They were probably already overcrowded. Anyway, what need had I of white beaches and golden sun, when Bozo and Big Betsy awaited me?

★ ★ ★

That was how I came to be driving along this narrow curving road that wound through rolling hills green with foliage and spring flowers, cut at dramatic

2

intervals by gashes of red soil and granite rock. I marveled at blackberry brambles and spangles of Cherokee roses that draped the red earth, and the glistening white of the flowering dogwood that gave the impression of snow lingering beyond its season. There were crab trees bursting with riotous blossoms from delicate white to deep, deep pink. Wild honeysuckle provided a gay carpet of scarlet and orange and rose. The air, after that of New York City, smelled sweet with the heady fragrances of shrubs and flowers.

Surrounded by all this beauty, it was difficult to make myself face one unpleasant fact: I was lost. Pam's careful directions had brought me this far, to Dog's Leg Road, but the drive leading up to the Andrews house was to be a mile or so along this road, and I had traveled that far and more with still no sign of a driveway.

I saw a man clambering down one of the hills. I stopped the car, thinking he might be able to give me directions. He saw me, hesitating briefly before he finished his descent to stand by the side of the road. I got out of the car and started toward him.

He was quite tall, and lean — too thin, almost, with a tensed, keen look — I thought of the long, thin blade of a fine sword — and strikingly good-looking, with a well sculpted face and a mouth deep and straight.

'Hello,' I said. He nodded, showing neither welcome nor coolness; only waiting.

'I'm afraid I may be lost. I'm looking for a place called Home Acres. Do you know where it is?'

He stared full at me. His eyes were deep-set, and of a hard and brilliant blue. He smiled all at once, softening the hard lines of that handsome face. 'Why do you want to go there?' He had a soft, deep voice, with that southern hill accent that fondled each vowel into two sounds and slithered over the consonants as if they, hard and jangling, didn't matter much.

His question was impertinent, so that, without thinking, I stiffened and said rather curtly, 'Because it's where I want to go. Do you know where it is?'

4

Far from annoying him, my sharp reply only seemed to amuse him, which certainly did nothing to quell my impatience. Fresh from New York City, I was thinking: country bumpkin, no manners, never mind that he's handsome as the devil.

'It's just around that bend.' The drawl was thicker than ever, so that 'bend' because almost two separate words. He pointed down the road to where it twisted about an outcropping of rock. 'You can't miss it.'

He brought his hand back to his side and stood looking down at me, grinning in that annoying way. There was something mischievous in his manner that grated on my sensibilities. He wore jeans, faded until they were hardly blue at all, but a misty gray-white, and a shirt open nearly to the waist, revealing a lot of deeply tanned muscles. It was warm and he had been climbing, so that his body glistened in the sunlight with sweat. He looked altogether — irritatingly — masculine.

A bird broke from a tree with a loud

cry, swooping up toward the sun. I realized I was staring, saying nothing, and the moment had become long.

'Thank you.' I turned and went back toward my little Honda. I could sense his eyes on me, and they made me feel graceless, trying to walk on an unpaved country road in heels that threatened with each step to send me sprawling.

I don't know which was worse — that long walk to the car, sure that he was staring, or the discovery, when I got there and turned around, that he had disappeared and hadn't been watching me at all.

With a gesture of impatience, I got into the car and started it up again. I rounded the next curve and found the drive, as he had said. It was marked with crude pillars of heaped up stones, surmounted by a weathered old sign reading 'Home Acres.' Beyond the gateposts ran an avenue of cedars, leading up a rise. My sense of adventure, flagging before, quickened again. I forgot for now my encounter with that strange young man and thought only of what lay ahead.

I came over the rise, driving slowly, and had to stop. I was expecting to approach a little house hidden among the hills, but there below me stood a veritable plantation manor house, a splendid white structure poised in perfect symmetry. Its wide verandas with their French windows, its towering columns, its sprawling roofs, all seemed to belong to another world and another time.

Pam had told me the Andrews home was lovely. A little yellow house in the suburbs, with white shutters and a few shrubs, can be lovely. Here was more than mere beauty of line and form — here was the charm and grace that epitomized the Old South. One could almost see the curving drive lined with carriages. Elegant ladies, their skirts ballooned with crinolines, nodded and smiled at one another, while children played with hoops and jacks beneath the magnolia trees. And all Pam had said was, 'The Andrews home is lovely.'

Well, Pam was less a romantic than I. To her it was probably only an example of antebellum architecture, whose various parts she would name for me if I asked. She knew the working parts of every-thing, people included. She could list not only feet and hands and fingers, but each complex and neurosis and motivational force, without ever remembering the color of anyone's eyes.

Dear Pam. I was twenty-two and she only nineteen, so chronologically she was my young sister, but in every other respect she was the older. And all of my romantic notions notwithstanding, it was she who was engaged to be married, although, sensibly, not until she had gotten her degree from college, and to none other than the same young man who would one day inherit all this; while I, the romantic, had lately found the word 'spinster' sticking on my tongue.

I had just started to get out of the car when there was a loud yell and Pam ran down the wide steps toward me, her dark hair flying and her glasses slipping precariously down her nose.

'Chris!' she cried, and I cried at the same moment, 'Pam!' and we ran into one another's arms, laughing and squealing and acting like a couple of kids.

'It's so wonderful seeing you.'

'And you,' I said. 'And all this. Pam, it's fabulous. I had no idea.'

'Oh, the house.' She crinkled her nose. 'It's falling apart. If the South ever rises again, they'll need a major housing boom to start.'

She was right, of course. The house *was* falling apart. At a distance it had been stunning in its beauty, but the grounds, at a closer look, were poorly tended. The front of the house had been recently painted, but one wing was still gray with age. One of the chimneys had lost some bricks, which lay un-retrieved upon the roof, and at least one window upstairs displayed a broken pane of glass.

'You aren't going to Florida?' Pam asked with altogether too casual an air.

'Undecided. I've got a full month so I thought I could spare a few days to stop off here. I'll put myself up in the local inn if they have one.'

'You'll do no such thing. I've already told Mrs. Andrews you were coming and

9

you're to stay here as long as you like. You've got the room next to mine. We have no shortage of rooms.'

'It's enormous.'

'This place wears on my nerves, if you want the truth, but you'll love it, romantic that you are.'

We had come into a hall, bigger in itself than my entire apartment in Manhattan, floored in black and white marble and dripping crystal and gilt which reflected in a dozen or so mirrors along the walls. In the center was a great round table with claw feet, and atop it an urn of flowers in artless profusion. Beyond the table, a wide staircase sloped upward in a gentle curve. I looked up, counting three rows of galleries.

'And to think, someday this will all be yours.'

'Not for decades.' She lowered her voice to a conspiratorial whisper. 'Mrs. Andrews will live to be three hundred, if I'm any judge. Pioneer stock, you know.'

I laughed. From anyone else, that remark would have sounded dreadful, as if Pam were ardently coveting the place, or resented Mrs. Andrews's longevity, but I knew full well that Pam had little if any interest in becoming mistress here, and that she was rather fond of her future mother-in-law.

'Speaking of whom,' I said, 'isn't she here?'

'In a little while. She always lies down after lunch, but she should be down shortly. She said I was to greet you for her and make you feel at home. Have you eaten, by the way?'

'I stopped on the road, thanks, but I'll have some coffee if there is any. Which way is the kitchen?'

'Lord, I'm not sure I could find my way there, and even if I could, we wouldn't be welcomed. There's a dragon-faced lady by the name of Mrs. Maywood who's in charge there, and she brooks no . . . oh, hello.'

She was looking beyond me, over my shoulder. I turned and guessed from Pam's disconcerted manner and the newcomer's coolness that the woman standing in the open door was Mrs. Maywood.

'Mrs. Maywood,' Pam said brightly,

recovering, 'this is my sister, Christine Collins.'

Mrs. Maywood had been watching us with a cold stare — but that expression was like one of warm hospitality in contrast to the reaction that Pam's introduction produced. The old woman actually seemed to shrink away from us. Her eyes, dark and wide, grew wider still. I had an impression that only years of rigid self-discipline enabled her to remain where she was instead of fleeing.

Yet with all the violence of her reaction, she said nothing. Her lips were shut in a tight, thin line that grew tighter still.

I was too embarrassed and startled myself to say anything, but Pam was rarely silent for long.

'Is something wrong?'

Mrs. Maywood gave her head a violent shake and said in a shrill voice that threatened to break, 'No, miss.'

Assuming what I had always jokingly called her executive voice, Pam said, 'We'd like some coffee. Is there any?'

'Yes, miss, I'll bring some. Will there be anything else?'

12

Pam told her there would not, and Mrs. Maywood fled with an unmistakable air of relief.

'Well,' I said with an embarrassed little laugh, 'I know I'm not awfully pretty, but I had no idea that my appearance was so frightening.'

Pam did not appear amused. 'We're going to have a long talk,' she said in a low voice, 'later, when we aren't likely to be disturbed.'

I remembered that she had signed her letter Bozo, and looking now into her rather plain, honest face, I could see that something was bothering her. I was intrigued, but I knew better than to try to interrogate Pam. She'd tell me just what she thought I ought to know, and just when she thought I ought to know it, and until that time arrived, I might as well be patient.

I had a sweater over my shoulders. I slipped it off and said, 'I thought by now I would have met a few Melungeons.'

'They aren't allowed in the house.'

From Pam's letter, I had somehow put Melungeons in the same category as

ghosts and werewolves and other frightening but imaginary creatures. Pam's
matter-of-fact tone, however, did not
quite fit that picture.

'You don't mean they're real?'

'Oh, yes, they're real people.'

'But, the devil worship and the
bloodshed and all. I thought they were
like witches.'

'Witches were real, too, you know —
are real, for that matter. The question is
not whether one believes in witches,
because they did exist — people who
were called or who called themselves
witches. So did witchcraft. They did
do remarkable things. The question is
whether what they did was magic, or the
use of natural laws in ways not then
generally understood.'

'All right,' I agreed, remembering Pam
had done a paper on this subject in
school. 'What you're telling me is that the
Melungeons were real, too — some sort
of local bogeyman, but the bogey part
was made up?'

'Not entirely. The bloodshed was
certainly real; at least some of it was. As

for the devil worship, well, it's one of those things where history and myth have gotten all tangled up together till they can hardly be separated. It's quite fascinating, really, and very mysterious.'

I would have prodded her with more questions, because I did indeed find the subject fascinating, but we were interrupted by a sound from the hall. I turned in that direction, thinking Mrs. Maywood had returned with our coffee.

The woman who appeared in the doorway this time, however, was no servant. It took no witchcraft to identify her as the mistress of the house. Although she was short and plump, her erect carriage and the high tilt of her chin made her seem taller and more imposing than she otherwise would have been. She came into the room, pausing just inside, with the air of one very much at home in her kingdom.

'Ah, Pam,' she said, pausing to fix her steely gray eyes upon me. 'And this is your sister, Christine. Welcome, Miss Evans, to Home Acres.'

'Oh, dear,' Pam said, stepping into the

15

breach. 'I guess I wasn't very clear about that. I hardly ever think of it myself. Chris and I are only half-sisters, actually. Mrs. Andrews, may I introduce Christine Collins?'

My smile of greeting froze on my lips. It was disconcerting, to put it mildly, to have everyone that you met react with fear and astonishment, but there it was again. Mrs. Andrews, no less than Mrs. Maywood had been, was struck with fear at the very mention of my name. She held an elaborately carved silver-handled cane, and I could see that it trembled in her hands.

'One of *them*,' she said in a voice no more than a whisper. Then, as if she had been struck a violent blow, she gasped and sank to the floor in a dead faint.

2

It was certainly a dramatic beginning to my visit — and what, I found myself wondering, could I have expected in Florida, a flirtatious desk clerk?

Our coffee was entirely forgotten for the time being in the flurry of activity that followed. Mrs. Maywood appeared as suddenly and as silently as if she had been waiting outside the door for just such a thing to happen. In another moment or so, a second servant arrived, a girl whose name, I gathered from the conversation, was Annie; and on her heels, a slow-moving man in work clothes whose name, so far as the conversation told me anything, might have been 'You.'

Making up in exclamations of alarm what they lacked in efficiency, this task force soon had Mrs. Andrews off to her bedroom. More dismayed than I cared to show, I stood discreetly in the back-ground and wondered. It was frightening, this reaction that these people had to me, and completely puzzling as well. I could hardly be expected to feel welcome under the circumstances.

'And you are being a selfish prig,' I told myself when the others had gone. 'Mrs. Andrews might be seriously ill. That faint might have been a stroke or something of that sort, and here you are worrying about your wounded vanity.'

'I guess we'll have to forego the coffee,' Pam said when we were alone in the parlor again. 'How about a drink instead? There's some really nice sherry.'

'Oughtn't you to be with Mrs. Andrews?'

'Forgive me if I sound a little hard-hearted, but I've learned since I've been here that fainting is practically *de rigueur* with these ladies of the old school. When in doubt, drop to the floor.'

'It looked awfully authentic to me,' I said doubtfully. Pam was not a sentimental girl.

'Don't worry. In any event, Mrs. Maywood is with her and, take my word for it, she'd as soon we stay out of her way until she gets things running smoothly again. Believe me, when I even walk toward the dining room, she grabs the crystal to her bosom lest I should knock it to the floor.'

Pam had gone to a little table by the window. She poured sherry for both of us and brought mine across the room. 'I just wish Peter had been here to see it all. He'd fairly howl.'

'Isn't he here?' I sat in one of the massive chairs, its wings seeming to wrap themselves around me, and sipped my wine. I was not much of a drinker, but just now I thought it might do more good than harm. 'I was looking forward to meeting him.'

'Only if you stay around for a while. He's doing his thesis on the pre-Spanish explorers of North America, and he learned about some relics in a museum in Maine, so off he went. To tell the truth, I think he wanted to avoid any fireworks between his family and me. Not that there have been any yet, but just in case.'

'It looks as if all the fireworks were saved for my arrival,' I said in a gloomy voice.

'Poor Chris. You did give them a start, didn't you?'

I swirled the sherry in my glass. 'You know, I didn't get the impression it was me, exactly. Mrs. Andrews looked perfectly happy to see me until she heard my name. That was when everything snapped.'

'Oh, Lord,' Pam said, clapping a hand to her forehead. 'How absolutely stupid of me. That's it, of course. Your name is Collins.'

'Well, good heavens, yes, and has been as long as I can remember. What's so startling about that? Don't tell me that someone named Collins was the local axe murderer or some such thing?'

'It's every bit as bad. Maybe even worse, in Mrs. Andrews's eyes. Collins is a Melungeon name.'

I set the sherry aside with a clunk. 'That does it. Now you've got to tell me about those blooming Melungeons. If I've been named after one, I have a right to know, and I won't be put off, either, so don't try. I don't care if he was green and had horns in the middle of his forehead.'

Not that Pam looked as if she intended to put me off. Far from it, however; she looked positively delighted. 'It's really terrific,' she said, leaning forward in the way she had when she was truly interested in something. That was what I liked best about Pam — her lack of artifice. She might step on your toes if you didn't watch out — frequently did, in fact — but at least you knew just how she felt about anything.

'At first I thought it was charming simply because it was such a fun accumulation of monster stories, but actually it's much more than that. It's a genuinely fascinating historical mystery. Peter's been digging into the Melungeon legends for years. That's what got him started on this thesis of his on the pre-Spanish explorers. They're related subjects, you see.'

'Oh for heaven's sake, Pam, don't give me one of your classroom introductions. I thought they were awful creatures that gobbled up unsuspecting girls from above the Mason-Dixon line.'

'You won't joke about them with

people around here, I can tell you that much. Some of them still believe that if you're fool enough to wander into Melungeon country after dark and you get back without being shot, you're certain to wizen and perish with some ailment that nobody can cure.'

'Witchcraft?'

'More than that, though. To begin with, the Melungeons themselves are a puzzle. They are often, though not always, a dark-skinned people, and nobody knows where they came from. That's the mystery — or part of it, at any rate. There is evidence to suggest they might have been in the country a thousand years before Columbus. Peter thinks maybe longer than that, even. By the time the white settlers got to Tennessee, the Melungeons had long since settled all the good bottom land.'

'Pam, darling, wait. How on earth did they get to Tennessee, of all places? I mean, I can see a coastal region, or even along one of the major rivers, but here?'

Pam gave her head a shake. 'Nobody knows that, either. There's a Professor

Gordon of Brandeis who thinks that they're linked with the ancient Hebrews, one of the lost tribes of Israel. He hasn't any real theory for how they got to this country, but he thinks they did about fifteen hundred years ago, and that they somehow found their way through North Carolina and Virginia.' She grinned mischievously. 'I've talked to some of the Melungeons themselves — Lord, Mrs. Andrews would turn positively purple if she knew that — but they don't know much more than anybody else about their history. One of the women says she heard from an uncle that their people came from North Carolina, and she thinks they originated with deserters from De Soto's Spanish expedition of Fifteen-forty. Some historians do think he managed to reach what is now east Tennessee.'

'Spanish?' I thought for a moment. 'But the word Melungeon doesn't sound Spanish, does it? Or Hebrew. And for that matter, neither does the name Collins. I would have thought my name was of English derivation.'

'Yes, the word is a mystery, too. There's

a theory that it derives from the French word, *mélange*, meaning mixture, and another that it derives from the Afro-Portuguese *melungo*, meaning shipmate. That, at least, would tie in with another theory held by many Melungeons themselves, that the people are of Portuguese descent, somehow related to a long-ago band of shipwrecked sailors. And with a little imagination, some of the Melungeon names, like Collins, Mullins, Goins, and so on, can take on a Portuguese flavor — Collins, for instance, and Mollen.'

'Maybe,' I said, still not entirely convinced.

'There's plenty of other theories, too, if you don't like that one. One, for instance, that says they're descendants of Raleigh's colony at Roanoke. That disappeared in about fifteen-sixty, if you remember your history. And even the Phoenicians get their share of the credit, too.'

'All right,' I said, laughing lightly, 'I'll grant that their history is a puzzle, and a very fascinating one, but you haven't explained the devil worship and all the rest. Whoever they are, and wherever they come from, how did they become such monsters?'

'Well, that's much less mysterious, but pretty scary in its own way. I've already told you, when the white settlers got here, they found the Melungeons inhabiting the best lands. That didn't earn them any affection on the part of the new settlers, as you can imagine. Greed is an ugly business. And the Melungeons were, for the most part, a dark-skinned people — not Negroid, more Latin-looking, but certainly darker than the pale English settlers. The Melungeons had straight black hair, and different social habits, and they were inclined to stay off to themselves rather than mix with the newcomers.'

'I think I'm beginning to get the picture.'

'Exactly. They were the inevitable targets for prejudice; and, of course, the more the new settlers looked at those good bottom lands, the more prejudiced they became against the Melungeons. They began to pass laws. By this time, the Melungeons were a minority, and in no time at all, they couldn't vote or hold office or bear witness in court. It wasn't long before the Melungeons had been forced off their lands and driven onto the high ridges. The result was inevitable, too. You can imagine how the Melungeons felt, being treated so badly, robbed of their homeland. They began to make raids, burning and stealing — and the legends were born.'

'That's the way most of those myths start, isn't it — a little foundation in truth, and a lot of imagination? In this case, mixed generously with guilt and a justifiable fear.'

She nodded. 'Yes. There was undoubtedly some very real murder and bloodshed. The light-skinned settlers began to talk of devil worship and blood-drinking. You know, all the usual monster tales. Children boiled and eaten, so the Melungeons stories went, and heaven alone knows what else. In a short time, the Melungeons had become bogeymen to the people about here, and they have remained so ever since.'

'But surely today, in our enlightened society, people don't still believe in those

26

stories?' Pam was right in thinking the story of the Melungeons was fascinating in its way, but I could scarcely credit anyone in our time with being genuinely frightened of devil-worship and the sort of monster tales she was relating.

'People will give up almost anything else before they'll surrender their prejudices. You saw how Mrs. Andrews reacted, just to your name. Oh, Mrs. Maywood,' she said, standing abruptly. The servant had glided in as silently as before. 'How is Mrs. Andrews?'

'She's recovering.' She fixed her cold eyes on me and said, 'She's asked to see Miss Collins.' She spoke my name in a flatly disapproving tone. I could understand a little of what the Melungeons must have felt in their years of persecution.

'You will come with me, won't you?' I said to Pam. I knew that Mrs. Andrews was a harmless and probably a genuinely nice person, but after our first dramatic encounter, I could not help being a little uneasy about a second meeting.

Pam put no great stock in that sort of

timidity, however. 'If she had wanted me along, she'd have asked for the two of us. You go along. She probably wants to apologize for your poor welcome here, and she won't want me glowering over your shoulder.'

Pam was right, of course. Mrs. Andrews did indeed want to apologize, which she did profusely. She was propped up in bed with a mountain of pillows. The bed itself was a museum piece, with lush canopies and draperies at all four sides.

'You must think us dreadful,' she said, offering me her hand for all the world as if she expected me to kiss it. 'I'm afraid I've been under a strain lately, and when I heard your name . . . but that's rather a long story, too long to get into now.'

'Pam did explain a little. About the Melungeons.'

She gave me a sharp look. 'Did she? Her version, of course.' She sounded rather disinclined to trust Pam's version of the facts. 'Well, the real story can wait, in any case, until tomorrow. In the meantime, do forgive me, please, and I hope your stay with us will be pleasant despite its beginning.'

'I'm certain that it will be.'

'It was so silly of me,' she said, looking me over. 'You're so fair, and that blonde hair, and coming from New York. You could hardly be . . . ' She caught herself and gave a little wave of her hand, in which she clasped a lacy handkerchief. 'Ah, well, let it alone. Now you must excuse me, my dear. I think I shall rest.'

'Surely,' I said, standing. I wished her well and started from the room. As I turned from her bed, I was thinking that before I had come up to her room, I had been undecided as to whether I would be staying or not, but in my conversation with Mrs. Andrews, that had been taken for granted.

And why not, I thought. I had nothing better to do. It was a lovely old home in a romantic setting, and beset with mysterious and frightening, if actually harmless, legends.

Mrs. Andrews, however, did not consider the legends harmless. I was reminded of that as I reached the door and she called after me, 'Miss Collins?' I turned and with an uneasy little smile, she asked, 'Your family didn't come from Tennessee, did they?'

'I'm afraid not,' I said, returning her smile. 'We're northerners as far back as anyone has dared to look.'

She bade me good day then, and I went out, but I knew why she had asked. The possibility that I might have Melungeon blood in me, fair skin and blonde hair notwithstanding, had lingered in her mind.

Nor had that smile she had given me hidden the fear in her eyes. The old woman's elegance and charming manners could not quite conceal the fact that she was frightened out of her wits.

★ ★ ★

I came down to find that Pam was no longer in the room where I had left her. Mrs. Maywood had disappeared also, presumably into the kitchen.

I went out into the hall. The front door was ajar and I went outside. There was no sign of her there, either but I found that my things had been removed from the car, so she had been busy getting me settled in.

It was sunset. The sky had gone pink and gray behind the hills to the west. I found myself thinking again what a beautiful place I was in. The hills were a hundred different shades of green, dappled here and there with flecks and bits of color from flowers and blossoms. A bird sang happily from a tree somewhere nearby, and from a hedge in the distance his mate replied.

In no hurry to be back inside, I strolled idly about the house, admiring the view, enjoying the peace and quiet, so different from evening in Manhattan with its squeal of tires on pavement and subway rumbles.

The lawns stretched smoothly back for a few hundred feet and were bordered by white fences, beyond which grew tall grasses and shrubs and trees that thickened and became a wood as they moved further away. Beyond that the hills rose up, gently at first and then more steeply, to form a backdrop. A murmuring of water told me there must be a creek not too far distant. Little wisps of mist swirled through the ravines.

I strolled toward the rear, pausing to study a ring of brown earth that stood out in the green of the grass. It was almost a perfect circle, and though the grass was green and lush at its edge and in its center, in the band itself, which was perhaps eight inches wide, there was not a blade. It looked eerily unnatural.

A voice behind me said, 'It's a devil's dance.'

I started and looked, and saw nothing. The voice might have come from the mist filtering through the distant trees.

'I see you found the house.'

This time I realized it came from above, and I looked up into the branches of a magnolia tree. I saw him then, sitting on one of the branches — the young man from the road who had given me directions for finding the house.

'Oh,' I said, letting out the breath I had been holding, 'it's you.'

'Who did you think it was? A devil?'

'I didn't think at all. What are you doing up there, anyway?'

'Sittin'.'

'I can see that much, but why up there, where no one can see you?'

'Because I'm not supposed to be seen. Not here, leastways.'

'Oh.' I saw at once what he meant. The Andrewses were undoubtedly high up in the local social hierarchy, while this poor creature, handsome though he was, was obviously nothing more than a country lout. It was easy to imagine that he had, at some time past, made a pest of himself, perhaps hanging around the kitchen door looking for handouts — or maybe flirting with that girl, Annie. Certainly he was the sort to turn a girl's head — and had to be forbidden to come around. So he must hide himself in trees in order to have a glimpse of this splendid house and the elegant way of life it no doubt represented to him.

Poor dear, I found myself thinking. An accident of birth had trapped him here, as surely as if he were tied to that magnolia tree; while I, through no good grace of my own, had been born to an entirely different way of life.

I glanced about, and my eyes came back to the ring of brown earth, so conspicuous in the green grass. 'What did you call this?'

'A devil's dance. It's where the spirits come at night, in the moonlight, to dance in a ring.'

He said it lightly, but I had a feeling, reinforced by my interview with Mrs. Andrews, that these hill folk took such legends rather more seriously than not. I said, trying not to sound patronizing, 'Have you ever seen them dancing?'

His eyes grew wide, like a frightened little boy's, and he gave his head a violent shake. 'Mercy, no. If you see them, and they invite you to dance, it means you're going to die.'

I was fortunately saved the necessity of replying to that observation by the sound of Pam's voice, calling to me: 'Chris?'

'Here,' I called back, and turned to see her coming across the lawn toward me. I glanced once into the magnolia tree, but the feet that had dangled just over my head had disappeared, and I recalled that the young man was not supposed to be here at all. Why I should care whether he was found trespassing, I had no idea, but quite instinctively I moved away from the tree and went to meet Pam.

'Were you talking to someone?' she asked.

I shook my head. 'No. Singing under my breath, maybe. I was just admiring the lovely setting.'

She gave me a curious look, as if she did not quite believe me, but she let it go. 'It is lovely, isn't it?'

'Is that what they call a devil's dance?' I asked, pointing at the ring of brown earth.

'What? Oh, that, yes. It's one of the country legends about dancing demons and dying. If you hear the piping, or see the devils, it means you're going to die. I suppose the truth is that the soil right there lacks nitrogen.'

We had started slowly back toward the house. Pam was not one to be frightened by legends. To her mind, there was a sensible and scientific explanation for everything — which might well be true, but it was a point of view that I thought robbed life of a great deal of romance.

'But, just in that ring?' I said thoughtfully, looking back. 'Isn't that peculiar?'

'How did you know it was called that anyway? I'm quite sure it isn't a New York legend.'

'Oh, I don't know. Something I heard, I suppose. Someone must have told me about it at some time or other.' I glanced back toward the magnolia tree, but there was no sign of human life in its branches and I could not tell if he were still there, or had gone. Perhaps, I thought, smiling a little to myself, he had never been there. Maybe he was only one of the spirits of the ring, and had been about to ask me to dance.

Except, he did not at all appear to be a wicked angel. Mischievous — surely he was that — but not really wicked. He did have something of the wood sprite about him, though. One could easily imagine him dancing in a glade, or playing sly jokes on unwary travelers.

My thoughts paused in their circling. What jokes might he have been playing upon me? None that I could see. He had given me the right directions for finding the house and he had told me the correct legend of the devil's dance, because Pam had said much the same thing. Yet, looking back, I had a sudden memory of a mischievous smile. Had he been playing some joke on me?

3

I realized guiltily that Pam had been talking as we walked, while I had been lost in my reveries.

' . . . think you'll be completely comfortable there,' she said. 'It's in the back, but it has a splendid view of the hills.'

'I don't think there'll be much of a view, with this mist rising. Is that common?'

'Fairly.' The faint mist had become a genuine fog, creeping closer to the house in little gusts of gray. 'Usually it's not this bad, but if there's a really warm day, and the temperature drops sharply at night, it may get awfully thick. We had a bad fog just a couple of nights ago; you truly couldn't see your hand in front of your face.'

I shivered involuntarily. 'Somehow one doesn't associate that sort of thing with the hills of Tennessee.'

'It's wild country still.' She led the way up the stairs and along the upstairs hall.

'Is there any danger from wild animals?'

'Some. Of course there are plenty of snakes — rattlers and copperheads. The locals say cases of snakebite are rare, but with names such as Copperhead Cove, one does wonder. And there are bears.'

'Bears? Grizzlies?'

'Black bears, and only a minimal hazard. If you meet one on the trail the best thing is just to stand still. They'll charge at you as if they mean to attack, but they stop just before they get to you.'

'Pam! You don't for a minute think I'm going to stand still while some bear is charging at me?'

She laughed. 'Well, chances are you'll never see one. They do try to avoid humans, so sightings of them are rare. And there are packs of wild dogs, too, I hear, although I haven't seen any of them. They say they will attack small animals or children, but I doubt that an adult would be in any danger.'

I gave an involuntary shudder. 'It all

looks so harmless and bucolic, but you make it sound like a sea of dangers.'

'Actually, there's little to worry about. I've been out in the woods time and time again, and I've yet to meet anything more dangerous-looking than one or two cheerless old farmers. The important thing is to watch where you step, lest you disturb a sleeping rattler. Carry a stick with you when you go out, and poke around in front of yourself. You'll be safe enough. Anyway, look at it this way — you're in no danger of being mugged.'

I had to laugh with her. It was true; there were probably more dangers per square mile in my hometown Manhattan than in those mist-covered hills beyond this house. Snakes, wild dogs, even bears would probably avoid me if given any chance to do so, but the predators that prowled that urban wilderness were more likely to seek me out to do their damage.

We had come to a room at the end of the hall. 'I think you'll be comfortable here,' she said. She said it, though, with a certain dry irony. She was not of so thoroughly a practical mind that she did not understand my romanticism, and she knew full well I would find the room enchanting.

There was a heavy, old-fashioned sofa that would never do for my little city apartment, but that made this cavernous room seem cozy. This was a big room, and old, with the same ivory walls as the hall and the same oak flooring covered with old but obviously fine Bokhara rugs. An enormous bed stood against one wall, canopied and hung with a charming chintz that only partially offset its massive size. A blue basin and jug stood on a chest across from the bed, although those items were no longer necessities as they would have been in the past. There was a copper kettle, too, genuinely old and battered, and filled now with purple and yellow pansies.

The windows were the French style, long and latticed and just now open, so that some of the mist that had taken over the gardens by this time had drifted in; but with it came the sound of the wind in the trees and the scent of pine and honeysuckle and wisteria and, ever so faintly, of moss.

'It's beautiful. I used to read about the Old South when I was a little girl, and dream myself into rooms like this.'

Pam went across to shut the French windows. 'Well, I'm sure in your dreams they didn't have this crazy mist. It looks like it's going to be thick as pea soup tonight, and make everything creaky and musty. I'll have someone light a fire for you. We need them here right up to the dead of summer.'

I sat on the edge of the bed, testing its firm springiness, and gave a little delighted laugh. 'Oh, Pam, it's so good to be here.'

She came over to lay a hand on my shoulder. 'I'm glad you like it.'

'To think I could have been in Florida, in an ordinary hotel room, instead of this.' I indicated the room with a sweep of my hand.

'Don't dismiss Florida so lightly,' she said wryly. 'It does offer certain advantages.'

'Such as?' I would not give up my eager

enthusiasm. I jumped to my feet and went across to the French windows. The fog had indeed taken over outside. I could see a balcony, the wisteria's purple blossoms tumbling over its railings, but beyond that there was little more than a curtain of gray. The sun had set, and it was as if the mist had only waited for that to proclaim its authority over the land.

'Eligible young men, for one thing.' Pam turned the lamps on to give the room a warm glow.

'And there aren't any here?'

'Not a one. I've checked it out thoroughly. They go away as soon as they're old enough, and they don't come back until they've seen the world and are fifty-ish at least. With the exception of Peter, there isn't a young man in forty miles between the ages of eighteen and fifty who isn't already married and gone to fat. And Peter, I may remind you, is spoken for.'

'Well, I'll remember that. And lucky he is, but you must be putting me on. Surely there's one handsome young woodsman, someone tall and dark and rugged, with a lean, spare look.'

'A few tall and dark, but not hand-some, and not lean. And except for Jamie MacBride, who is three hundred pounds if he's an ounce, none who are single.'

I turned back to the windows and the mist beyond, swirling into mysterious forms, only to break and reform itself in a moment. One thing was certain: my young man from the road and from the magnolia tree was not Jamie MacBride, not by a great many pounds, and he was certainly over eighteen, and well under fifty, and although he might well be married — men here probably did not always wear wedding rings when they were married — no one could possibly call him fat.

'Do you suppose there really are spirits out there? Demons, perhaps, who can assume human forms pleasing to us?'

'If there are, I'm afraid I haven't seen them; but if anybody would, it would be you, wouldn't it, my romantic little sister?'

'Yes, I suppose it would,' I said, remembering the mischievous look on the

44

handsome stranger's face. Was that why he had been laughing?

Somewhere below, a hound began suddenly to bay. His howling came up through the mist with an eerie, discomforting quality that seemed to bode ill for the future.

★　★　★

I woke in the morning to the singing of a bird and the golden sunlight flooding through the latticed windows. The sky was so clear and so blue that it gave a lie to the mists of the night before, and you could easily wonder if you had only imagined them. This golden morn, with breath all incense and cheek all bloom, had certainly laughed the clouds away with playful scorn.

I had just risen when a tap came at the door and, at my call, the young woman I had seen yesterday came in. She hesitated inside the door, one hand still on the knob, and cast a sideways glance at the bed.

'Good morning, Annie,' I greeted her.

'Morning,' she said. Not a trace of a smile brightened that otherwise pretty face. Except for her stolid cheerlessness, I could certainly imagine my phantom friend of yesterday courting her, but I somehow rather supposed he would choose someone with a bit more spirit. On the other hand, where pickings were slim . . .

'Are you up?' she asked.

I patently was, of course, but I had already been warned: 'She's slightly retarded,' Pam had said of the girl the night before. 'Not seriously, of course; just a bit slow-witted. She's bright enough for the housework. You feel like you want to help her, but she doesn't exactly encourage friendliness. Well, you'll see for yourself.'

'Yes, you may go ahead with the bed, if you like,' I said, trying with my own smile to coax one out of her.

It was an unsuccessful attempt, though. Her face remained stubbornly expressionless as she came in and began to make up my bed. I had promised myself that I would try to be friends with her. It was hardly surprising that she should resent those around her whose minds could encompass so much more than hers could. She was probably smart enough to know her limitations, and be unhappy with them.

I thought it best, however, not to push matters. By showing her that I wanted to be friendly, and allowing her time to comprehend that fact, I would probably succeed where more aggressive action would fail. I left her to her chores and went to the window to look out over the hills, still gleaming with dew in the morning sun.

'Like a maiden, glancing o'er her pearls,' I said aloud.

I had forgotten already Annie's handicap. She asked, 'What?' in a thick, slow voice.

'Nothing,' I said, embarrassed by my tactlessness. 'I was just quoting someone else.'

'My ma says talking to yourself is crazy.' With that pronouncement, she turned her back on me again and went back to her work.

Thus chastised, I thought it best to dress for the day and save getting acquainted with Annie for a more auspicious occasion.

Mrs. Andrews certainly had not chosen her household servants for their good cheer, what with the dour Mrs. Maywood and Annie's lack of spirit. I began to understand why, lovely as this place was, Pam had not been entirely happy here by herself, and had longed for me to come, if only for a visit. Peter was away, the servants were unfriendly, and Mrs. Andrews herself, for all her southern charm, was probably not the ideal companion for someone of Pam's practical and intellectual nature.

There was something more, too — something vague and difficult to put into words, especially now in the golden light of morning; but I had felt it last night, with the room edged in mist and a dog howling somewhere in the distance. There was a brooding aura of — not quite danger, that was probably putting it a bit strongly — but of malaise; a threatening scent in the wind. I knew Pam felt this too, despite the fact that she had pooh-poohed it when I questioned her last night.

'There isn't actually anything amiss,' she had insisted. 'Not really. I was lonesome, and frankly, I find this place depressing with Peter not around.'

Annie finished her work and left. I was just putting a ribbon in my hair when Pam came into my room.

'It's fantastic,' she said, watching while I tied the bright blue ribbon, 'you've been here less than twenty-four hours and already the place seems brighter and gayer than it did.'

'It's all those woods spirits, coming around to have a look at me.'

'Not, I hope, the spirit of Big Betsy. I don't think the house could take that.'

I clapped my hands delightedly. 'Big Betsy! I had forgotten. You must tell me about her.'

'I'm starving. Couldn't Big Betsy wait?'

I planted my feet firmly and crossed my arms over my bosom. 'I mean to fast until you tell me all about Betsy.'

'All right,' Pam said, relenting with an

affectionate sigh, 'but let's at least compromise. I'll tell you on the way downstairs to breakfast.'

'Fair enough.'

'Big Betsy was known as the she-devil moonshine queen, and there are a great many lurid tales about her,' Pam said as we went. 'She sold moonshine whiskey, of course — apparently some pretty good stuff, and it was said she dealt in witchcraft and spells, too. That was one of the reasons she was never arrested over the whiskey business. People were afraid of her.'

'One of the reasons?' I cocked an eyebrow.

'The other one, far less romantic, is that she was simply too fat.'

'Too fat,' I repeated, expecting anything but that.

'They were afraid they wouldn't be able to get her out of the house, let alone down the hill. From what I've learned talking to people who remember her, it seems she was really a very kind old lady, quite harmless, but something of a recluse. She lived in a crude cabin way back in the hills, and she grew to be enormous, some say as much as six hundred pounds. Probably she suffered from elephantiasis, but the people then wouldn't likely have had that word in their vocabulary.'

'It sounds very sad.'

'But even that was against her, don't you see? Because it made her all the more a freak, and thus something to be feared.'

'How lonely life must have been for her.'

'Yes, and when she did die, they had to remove part of a wall just to get her out of the house. They wrapped her in quilts and rolled her, very gently I'm told, down the hill to be buried.'

'And I suppose now they say her spirit still haunts the hills.'

'The people around here have a plethora of spirits that haunt the hills, Betsy's among them; but her ghost, at least, ought to be recognizable by its size.'

Mrs. Andrews waited for us in the dining room, looking quite recovered from her fainting spell. 'So unfortunate, your having a name like that,' she said in a tone only mildly chastising. 'Of course, you couldn't help it, one supposes.'

However, having shown me that I had been inconsiderate to choose a name like Collins, Mrs. Andrews seemed satisfied that the matter was ended, and she set herself to being charming — a southern art that she had plainly mastered. Although much of her conversation was trivial and lacking in substance, there was a great deal of it, and its sweetness blended well with the hot biscuits and fresh butter that Mrs. Maywood brought in from the kitchen. Indeed, Mrs. Andrews's approach to life was a jelly rather than a bread-and-butter one, and while too much of her would be tiresome, one could not help enjoying a sampling.

'This jam,' Mrs. Andrews said, handing me a pot of red-colored jam when I had been about to use another, 'is the best. It's from the raspberries just up our hill in back. Mrs. Maywood picks them herself, and makes the jam. Laura May Hollis makes raspberry jam, too, but hers isn't as good as this. Nobody's is. I must have Mrs. Maywood pack you up some to take back to New York with you. It must be very hard to get decent food there. Store-bought things are never as good, I always say. I'll have Mrs. Maywood fetch you a ham to take along, as well. Our hams are better than those Kentucky ones. My daddy taught us to throw a little dogwood on the fire with the hickory. It gives it a special flavor.'

Across the table, Pam rolled her eyes.

'That's very kind of you, and I'd love to take some jam home with me,' I said, quite sincerely. The prattle notwithstanding, it was delicious jam. 'But it would be wasteful for me to take a whole ham. Perhaps a slice?'

'Nonsense. You just hang it in a cool place and it'll keep forever. The cellar would be very nice.'

I smiled and nodded, and tried not to think of what my building manager would say should he find a ham hanging in our basement laundry room. Assuming, of course, that it stayed there long enough for him to see it. But Mrs. Andrews's goodness was of such a determined sort that it was folly to attempt to argue with it.

'Do you do much farming here?' Behind the house, stretching into a wedge between two hills, was a fenced field planted with what looked like corn, but it had been too small and too far away for me to be certain.

'Ours is the best farmland around here. The very best. It's belonged to our family for generations, and when Nathaniel, my late husband, bless his soul, was alive, we farmed several hundred acres here and over in the hollow. But since he left me — that will be five years this fall — I have cut back on everything, because there was no one to run it for me except Peter, and he was away at school, and Jed, our hired man, but he's just too slow and too thickheaded to run a real farm. So now we have a little corn and a garden patch, just what we'll use ourselves, and a little extra. I wish I could tell you how people have fussed at me to grow more of our melons, because they are the best melons you can get — everyone says so — but we raise just enough for ourselves now, and a few friends. I must have Mrs. Maywood fetch you a melon or two to take home, there should be some ripe by the time you go.'

Pam said with a sober face, 'You could hang them in the cellar, with the ham.'

'Yes, yes, a good idea,' Mrs. Andrews agreed brightly, bobbing her head up and down.

I shot Pam a frosty look and sipped my coffee, which was, I was assured, the very best coffee, because Mrs. Maywood ground the beans herself and had a secret recipe. I was to be given a package of this to take with me when I went. I saw that I should not need to shop for foodstuffs for quite a while after my return to New York.

Breakfast over, Pam gave me a tour of the place. 'I would go with you,' Mrs. Andrews said, 'but I find that I must rest after a meal. I'm no longer in my springtime, you know.'

We left her and made our way slowly through the house, even invading Mrs. Maywood's kitchen.

'If she comes after us with a knife,' Pam whispered in the hall, 'We'll run in different directions.'

There were no attempts on our lives, however, although our appearance earned us frosty looks from the housekeeper, who at once went back to stirring a large kettle at the stove. Annie was there, too, and I paused to admire the polishing job she was doing on a silver teapot. She was, as usual, uncommunicative to a degree that bordered on sullenness. Again, I felt a sense of resentment toward me.

'Is that the real color of your hair?' she asked me out of the blue.

'Why, of course,' I said. She stared hard at my butter-colored hair and, without thinking, I said, 'It's not much lighter than your own.'

One close glance at her hair, however, told me that yellow was not her real color. It was bleached, and not terribly well. It seemed to me a pathetic attempt at glamour, and another reason for her to resent me. True, it was a trivial reason; but then, her thinking was limited, and it might seem a very important thing to her.

She did not seem to notice my faux pas, though. She dismissed me by returning her attention to the teapot, and abruptly turning her back on me.

'She's certainly a strange girl, isn't she?' I said when Pam and I were in the hall again.

'Hmm, your wounded bird instinct coming to the fore, I suppose. But I think you're up against it there, Sis. It isn't only a question of being slow. She doesn't like people, period. Believe me, I've tried being friendly with her, but there's no response. No matter how nice you are, you always feel she'd as soon see you in your coffin.'

We went outside. In addition to the house itself, there were several outbuildings — stables, although horses were no longer kept, and a barn, largely filled with rusting equipment. 'But the best equipment,' Pam said in an imitation of Mrs. Andrews's thick drawl.

There was a smoke house, a summer kitchen, and a cool spring house where perishables would once have been kept, with a little stream, scarcely more than a finger of water, running through it. There were kennels as well in which there were, as nearly as I could count, a dozen dogs of great variety.

'Mr. Andrews did a lot of hunting, I gather,' I said.

'And Peter likes to take them out running when he's here. Although, truthfully, I don't think he'd have the heart to shoot a rabbit.'

'More credit to him.'

The field behind the house was indeed planted with corn, just getting a good start. The rows stretched back to two low hills and partway up one of them.

'At one time you could hardly walk all the way across the Andrews property, so I'm told,' Pam said. 'Of course, much of it was taken from the Melungeons.'

'I didn't realize that.'

'From what Peter tells me, the Andrews family must have been among the worst persecutors of the Melungeons. They got a lot of very valuable land out of it, but they came in for a large share of the bloodshed as well. They were targets over the years for a lot of blood vengeance.'

'That explains why Mrs. Andrews is so

sensitive about them. It's probably partly guilt, and of course, a once very justifiable fear that has carried down through the family.'

'She really believes the family is haunted by the Melungeons, and that they mean to finish off the Andrews clan, presumably by ghostly means. The poor dear. A floorboard can't creak at night without frightening her half out of her wits.'

'And that explains, too, why she was so overcome when she thought she had a real live Melungeon in the house, and your sister to boot. That must have been a real shock. And yet, that is all so long ago, surely.'

'Is it?'

'Isn't it?'

'Mrs. Andrews is still quite terrified. To her, it is very much something of the here and now.'

'But she can't have been like that all along. That sort of fear would drive a person bonkers in the long haul. No one could live with it indefinitely. Something must have happened, and recently, to frighten her so and bring all this ancient history to life again. What could it have been, do you suppose?'

We had been sitting atop the rail fence surrounding the cornfield. Pam looked as if she were about to answer me; then, she jumped down suddenly and brushed off the back of her skirt.

'We'd best go back in. Peter's supposed to call this morning. I almost forgot, and he'll be in a tizzy if he gets stuck with Mrs. Maywood at long distance rates. Extravagance is not that man's middle name.'

We went back to the house, Pam walking quickly and a little ahead of me. It was silly, and yet I had a notion that there was something Pam was hiding from me. I thought again of her letter to me in New York, signed with the name Bozo. Last night she had insisted that had been only an impulsive gesture resulting from her loneliness. I had a nagging feeling, though, that there was something more to it than that.

While we had sat on the fence talking, she held a little handkerchief in her hand,

and she held it still as she walked before me across the grounds; but in that few minutes since we had left the fence, she had tugged the piece of cloth nearly to shreds.

4

It was, all in all, a quiet day. I saw nothing of my mysterious young man. He seemed to have vanished, in true spirit fashion.

I did not mention him to Pam. I think I was a little afraid that if I did so, he would not appear again, like telling someone your wish prevents it from coming true. Though, of course, I was hardly wishing to see him again.

I did find occasion twice to wander out by the devil's dance in the grass, but there was no one hidden in the branches of the magnolia tree, and when I saw that I was provoking Pam's curiosity, I decided against further trips of that sort.

'I don't know why you're so fascinated by that circle of plain earth,' she said. 'It's really nothing so special. Sooner or later, one probably shows up on almost any lawn.'

'Maybe. I've never seen one before, though.'

'I rather think if we look in a plant encyclopedia, we can learn the reason for it.'

'I rather like the one I was given. I'd much rather think of spirits piping and dancing on the lawn than clanking about in chains in old houses.'

'I for one don't intend to go dancing when I go. I'd much rather a quick, quiet ceremony, a fire, and a dignified urn. It's much more practical.'

'Oh, well, if practicality were the answer to everything, there'd be no need at all for flowers or music or art. Or love, either, for that matter. I'm certain selective breeding is more efficient than the natural process.'

'Why not? It works well with cattle and dogs.'

'For one thing, we aren't dogs, although I have known a bitch or two over the years. And for another, has anyone ever really consulted the cattle about it, or the dogs?'

She giggled in a most impractical manner and launched into one of those lengthy descriptions of Peter which sounded just as silly and idolizing as if she were any romantic young woman in love, and not the cool and level-headed Pam she insisted upon being. I think everyone in love becomes a romantic, whatever their inclinations may be at other times.

Mrs. Andrews, at least, took a far less scientific attitude toward the devil's dance, which she heard us discussing at dinner.

'I wouldn't go there, if I were you,' she said, her shoulders drawing in as if in a chill wind. 'It isn't wise to tempt the devil.' She looked for a long moment into her glass of wine and when she spoke, I think she had gone far beyond our little conversation about the ring of earth on the lawn. 'Trouble's coming.' Her voice was dark with foreboding. 'I think he's coming over Hungry Hill right now, headed straight for this house.'

This was said with such intensity that it effectively stilled any other conversation. Pam and I could only stare silently across the table at one another. Something of Mrs. Andrews's grim anticipation had communicated itself to me, for I, too, suddenly had a vision of a dark spirit striding over the hills in the near distance, moving surely toward this house. Pam had always laughed at my flair for intuitiveness, but I had often had 'feelings' of what was to come, and they had rarely been wrong, and I wondered if this time could be an exception.

'Heavens,' Mrs. Andrews exclaimed, shaking off her mood of a moment ago, 'haven't we gotten gloomy? Will you have some more of this elderberry wine, dear? My beloved husband, Nathaniel, made this himself, from the very nicest berries.'

Mrs. Andrews stirred herself to be charming again, and for the moment her gloomy prediction was forgotten.

★　★　★

It rained that night, a gentle rain that seemed to slide down the curtain of night in little rivulets. There was no mist, and the morning broke golden and warm through gray clouds. Pam came early to my room.

'We're going hunting,' she declared while I dressed.

'We're going what?' I gave her a surprised look in the mirror.

'Hunting. For snakeheads.' She whirled out of the room, leaving me astonished.

I found her and Mrs. Andrews together at the breakfast table. 'Now, see here, Pam,' I said. 'To begin with, you know I am terrified of snakes. And anyway, I can't think what possible good snakeheads would be to anyone.'

She handed me a bowl of warm biscuits. 'We're going to have them for lunch.'

'Ugh,' I said, making a face, 'I don't think I could, not even to be polite.'

Mrs. Andrews put the tips of her fingers to her lips and tittered. 'Your sister is having fun with you. She means snakehead mushrooms.'

'What on earth . . . '

'Morels, in France,' Pam said, grinning too. 'They're quite a delicacy, and the season is just beginning. Mrs. Andrews is going to look for some for lunch, and she's agreed we can go along.'

'I ordinarily don't let anyone go with me,' Mrs. Andrews said. 'The mushrooms get rarer every year, and so many people think nothing of poaching, once they know where your hunting grounds are. But Pam will have to hunt them herself someday, and since you don't live around here, I don't think it can hurt to show you where I find them.' She said this in such a manner as to make me understand what a great exception she was making.

'It sounds fun,' I said, warming to their enthusiasm. It looked already like a fine day to be out in the woods.

'Laura May Hollis and her daughter, Nellie, are coming for lunch, especially to meet you,' Mrs. Andrews said. 'I've already warned them about your name, so you mustn't be embarrassed about that. It isn't something you could have helped, after all, short of changing it somewhere along the way.' She gave the impression that she rather thought that was what I ought to have done.

Pam rolled her eyes heavenward at the mention of Laura May Hollis. 'That woman is a crushing bore. Honestly, I think I'd rather die than to have to spend a day with her.'

'She likes you,' Mrs. Andrews said emphatically, as if that were a genuine surprise, 'and I do want to find some nice mushrooms. She can never find any really good ones. Mine are always the very best.'

* * *

'There's no exact date for the season,' Mrs. Andrews explained. 'Always spring, of course, usually after a rain, and when there's a gentle breeze blowing. The real mushroom-hunter knows by the feel and the scent of the air. Zeke will go with us.'

I expected a hired man, but Zeke, as it developed, was one of the hounds in the kennel: a tall, powerfully built creature whose dangerous looks were belied by his merrily wagging tail and his eager welcome. He greeted me with what I thought was a dash of condescension, seeming to realize at once that I was no experienced hunter; but he was not unfriendly, and with a disdainful toss of his head for his companions left behind in the kennel, Zeke took the lead and set off toward the woods.

It was spring at its most glorious. The woods were greenly veiled and there were ruby globes of bloom on the three-leafed stems of the trillium. I saw clusters of purple violets nestled against tree stumps and fallen logs, and delicate white Dutchman's breeches. The short green umbrellas of the May apple leaves had begun to unfurl, but the white, waxen flowers were still in buds.

We paused to admire a pale jack-in-the-pulpit in a mossy woodland cloister, and a yellow adder's tongue, which was far lovelier than its name suggested, with sharp, speckled leaves and flowers not unlike orchids.

On the hillsides, the blossoming redbud trees, now glowing pink, lighted up the dark thickets beyond the creek over which we crossed on flat rocks so perfectly spaced they might have been laid out by a landscaper. We passed an old apple orchard where the white-pink blossoms were showing already.

'One has to know what one is about,'

Mrs. Andrews said as we walked. 'They come up quickly, and may be gone in a few hours, and the season is short. It will end as soon as the weather turns hot and dry, and that could happen almost anytime. Watch out, now — they can be anywhere, although you're more likely to find them around old apple and elm trees.'

'It's called mychorrhiza,' Pam explained matter-of-factly. 'The relationship that exists between fungi and certain trees.'

'Oh, I wouldn't know about that. Nathaniel used to say you could smell them.' She did indeed seem from time to time to be sniffing the air.

Pam had carried a small paper bag with her, despite Mrs. Andrews warning that this was bad luck. 'They'll hide if they see that sack,' she said.

Pam, of course, refused to abide by that superstition, and pointed out that, unlike Mrs. Andrews, she had no pockets in her skirt, and without a sack she would be unable to bring home any mushrooms should we find them.

'We'll find them, have no fears,' Mrs.

Andrews said confidently. She strolled along, Zeke a few feet ahead of her, but staying close. Mrs. Andrews's head was bent and her eyes intent on the ground. I followed her example, but though I strained my eyes, I saw nothing.

We stopped at a fallen elm where it lay rotting. Mrs. Andrews pushed aside some leaves with the toe of her shoe. 'This will be a good spot for them someday,' she said, 'if they once get started. You must make note of this, Pam. Peter likes his spring mushrooms.'

We found none there, however, and went on to inspect a locust grove. 'We used to keep cows,' Mrs. Andrews said, 'and pasture them back here. One morning I noticed that one old cow ran straight for here as soon as they were put out, so I followed her, and sure enough, I found the stubs where she had nipped them off. So after that I wouldn't let them be pastured here, and do you know, that cow never forgave me. I couldn't get near her after that, but what she didn't try to kick me.'

She looked about as if to get her

bearings. 'Just about here,' she said, indicating a patch of ground with a wave of her hand. 'Yes, look.' She bent down with a triumphant expression and both Pam and I stooped with her. There, camouflaged against the background of matted and curled grass and leaves, was the fungus we were seeking. I had been expecting the white button mushrooms that one finds in supermarkets, but this was something quite different. It looked like a yellowish-brown sponge set on a stem, the whole growth about four inches high.

'They're out!' Mrs. Andrews exclaimed jubilantly. 'And not the snakeheads either, but the sponges.' She nipped the mushroom off close to the ground and shook it gently. 'To release some of the spores, so it will come back,' she explained, dropping the mushroom into the cavernous pocket of her skirt. I doubt that finding buried gold could have thrilled her more, and her excitement was infectious. I dropped to my knees, looking carefully about for another.

I gently pushed aside part of the

fragrant cover of leaves, looking for the mate to the one fine fellow she had found. For a moment, I saw nothing. Then my eyes grew accustomed to the protective coloring, and suddenly I saw them all about. They were like a forest of tiny brown Christmas trees, rising at odd angles out of the damp humus. Each brownish cap was a conical sponge intricately webbed with an irregular network of deep pits, and now, rather than blending with the background as they had done a moment before, they stood out against the leaves and forest debris like bas-relief figures in a woodland sculpture.

'These are *Morchella esculenta*,' Pam said, gathering them every bit as avidly as Mrs. Andrews and I were doing. 'The snakeheads are *Morchella conica*. They usually come a little earlier.'

I held one of the intriguing growths in my hand and studied it. 'Do I need to worry about poison?'

Mrs. Andrews snorted disdainfully and Pam said, 'Not with these. There's nothing poisonous that looks remotely like these. Mycophobia, the fear of mushrooms, is more superstition and folklore than anything else, as a matter of fact. Mushrooms have always been considered strange, unearthly things that spring up at night in the company of witches and elves, fairies and demons. When the spirits dance in that devil's dance that fascinates you so, Satan is said to sit astride a mushroom in the center. I don't know whether he's meant to be very small, or if the legends include a very large mushroom. These can grow rather large, but as far as I know, not large enough to serve as a chair.'

'But some mushrooms are poisonous, aren't they?'

'The *Amanita* genus, very rare, is the only fatal one. Oddly enough, apparently they are particularly delicious. There are tales of people exclaiming about how good they tasted, just minutes before they took sick. But, as I said, none of them look at all like this.'

Pam was rarely wrong in her facts, and I dismissed completely my fears regarding the mushrooms. We picked them for some time. It was a pleasant way to pass a morning. I liked the clear brook that we had to cross once more, its water bubbling and gurgling. I caught a glimpse of a rabbit jumping out of a briar patch, and quite as startled as I.

Although we talked little, there was an endless serenade to enjoy. We were treated to the wild trill of a cardinal singing, over and over, 'Pretty, pretty, pretty,' and the thrushes added their own comments.

I learned, too — fortunately, as our foray was drawing to an end — why we had brought Zeke with us. The big dog seemed content to loll about, sniffing in the thickets and giving brief, half-hearted chase to rabbits and squirrels. When we had filled our pockets and Pam's sack, and were ready to start back, Zeke again took the lead. We followed the stream for a distance. Zeke paused to sniff at a log, and since I was first on the path, I took the lead.

The big dog suddenly burst past me, bumping me and nearly knocking me over. I scarcely had time to be angry, however, for in the next instant he had closed his huge, powerful jaws upon a large snake only a foot or two ahead of me. It was coiled on the path, its coloration blending perfectly with that of the leaves and the grass, and I might very well have stepped right on it without ever seeing it.

We three stopped dead, Pam seizing my arm to hold me back, although there was not the slightest danger of my moving just then.

'A copperhead,' she said.

I did not have to be told the snake was poisonous, but he was no longer a threat. Zeke, with an ease that bespoke experience, had bitten the snake in half.

Mrs. Andrews was quite unperturbed. 'They sleep in sunny spots. With Zeke along, there's nothing to fear, but you could as well carry a stick and keep it poked out in front of you. There's really no danger, if you're sensible. The snake would rather avoid you, if he can.'

I assured her that I would do my best to keep the local reptiles happy, and we went on, but I was grateful now for Zeke's presence in the lead.

The walk in the woods, a diversion for Pam and me, had made the older woman sentimental. 'Nathaniel,' she said as we walked, 'knew all the things in the woods to hunt. He always carried them in his hat. Sometimes it was mushrooms, and sometimes it was the wild strawberries, so much better than the store-bought ones. Or it might be frosty ripe persimmons in the fall. He'd line his hat with fern fronds, so as not to stain it, and he would begin to holler as soon as he got to the barn lot. 'May Ellen,' he'd thunder, and you could hear him in the back pastures, 'Come see what I found!' He'd be as proud as a hunter getting a deer.'

She grew silent after that, and I saw by the set of her chin and the droop of her shoulders that she was tired. I thought again that someday soon Pam would be mistress of all this property. Would she remember where to find the mushrooms, or know where to pick the very best berries?

'The best,' 'the very best' — were those phrases part of the past, victims of a present in which 'good enough' reigned?

Did anyone really care any more about that extra soupçon of quality?

I knew Pam would say, 'Why invest the extra time, or money, or trouble, if it isn't getting you more nutrition or more use, something definable and tangible?' Perhaps she was right. She would marry Peter Andrews, they would pursue their careers and have a nicely working marriage, and they would be happy.

Alas, I felt certain too that she would never hear his voice thundering from beyond the barn, calling, 'Come see what I found!'

★　★　★

Laura May Hollis and her daughter, Nellie, came to lunch. They were birds of the same luxuriant feather, with pale faces and cheeks red with too much rouge, but they had in abundance that charm once so common to the South, and one did not greatly mind their china-doll quality, although I suppose it would be maddening to live with for long. We had sherry, and Mrs. Andrews told them, with not a little air of boasting, of our success in searching out mushrooms.

'It's important I show Pam these things,' she said. 'One of these days, I'll be with my Nathaniel, and the place will be Peter's — and hers, too, of course.'

Mrs. Hollis smiled at Pam, who had the air of one gritting her teeth for a long period of time. 'He'll be a fine husband, my dear. At one time he had his eye on my Nellie, but she was too young by far for him.'

Nellie, whose age I guessed to be perhaps a year less than Pam's, smiled.

'Why, Laura May Hollis, what a thing to say!' Mrs. Andrews exclaimed. 'He never had any such thing.'

'He did, he did. She practically had to drive him away from the place with sticks. And you, my dear,' Mrs. Hollis turned suddenly on me, before anyone could further dispute her version of the facts, 'have you no plans to get married?'

'Oh, yes, someday.'

Pam said, 'Chris is waiting for Prince Charming.'

'What's wrong with waiting for just the

right man, and knowing what you want?'

'And what sort of man is he?' Pam asked.

At that moment in our conversation, Mrs. Maywood came in to serve the mushrooms, and all enmity was forgotten in the enjoyment of their fragrant aroma. Mrs. Maywood had chopped and sautéed the mushrooms in butter, Mrs. Andrews informed me, and seasoned them with nothing more than salt and pepper.

'When you have the best mushrooms, you don't want to spoil them with a lot of fancy fixings,' she said, nodding her head sagely.

They were served up with crusty pan-fried steaks, mashed potatoes and warm, fluffy biscuits. The morels had a woodsy, spicy scent that brought to mind shining, rain-soaked leaves and damp mossy places, a scent of the earth that permeated their flavor.

I found them exceedingly delicious. Mrs. Andrews declared them the best she had ever picked, and Mrs. Hollis found them 'good,' with a certain grudging admiration in her voice.

Pam was the only dissenter. Mrs. Andrews saw that Pam had eaten less than half of hers. 'Why, Pam, dear, what's the matter with yours?' she asked.

'I'm not sure. There's something about them . . . '

'Are you saying they're bad?' Mrs. Hollis asked, a bit too eagerly.

'No, not bad. They're quite delicious, really. They just don't taste like morels.'

Mrs. Hollis nearly knocked her water glass over reaching across to get her fork into the chopped mushrooms on Pam's plate. She tasted, and positively beamed with triumph.

'They are off,' she said, smacking her lips. 'Very poor quality, I'd say.'

Mrs. Andrews, the quality of her mushrooms on the line, could do nothing but get up from her place and march around to Pam's, so that she could taste for herself of the questioned mushrooms.

'What nonsense,' she said fiercely — perhaps a trifle too fiercely. 'These are exactly the same crop. I can't think when I've ever tasted better mushrooms.'

'We had some day before yesterday that

were much better,' Mrs. Hollis said, obviously feeling that the initiative was hers now. 'Picked from our orchard.'

'I have been through that orchard of yours,' Mrs. Andrews said angrily. 'The mushrooms there are no better than toadstools. These,' and here, with a dramatic gesture, she heaped the rest of the offenders onto her fork and stuffed them into her mouth, 'are delicious.'

It was a gesture she was to regret. By mid-afternoon, Pam was deathly ill, and when I went in search of Mrs. Andrews to tell her, I found the poor creature, who had gone up for her nap after lunch, still abed, and growing sicker with each passing moment.

'Help me to sit up,' the old woman asked weakly, 'and fetch me the slop jar from under the sink, there. Then you must summon Doctor Williams. Mrs. Maywood knows how to get him. You must tell him to hurry; there's not a moment to lose. And when he is on the way, tell Mrs. Maywood we must have some milk thistle at once. She will know where it grows.'

She began to retch so violently that I thought the very effort of it must kill her, and as I held her heaving shoulders, I had a sudden, frightening realization of what it was.

Some intuition told me that the mushrooms on Pam's plate had been poisonous.

5

Mrs. Maywood, summoned by me, quickly took charge of Mrs. Andrews, leaving Pam to my care. In fact, there was little I could do, besides giving her a tisane made from the milk thistle Mrs. Maywood had hastily gathered. I remembered from first-aid instruction in school that the thing to do with poisoning was to make the person vomit, but in this instance, Pam had no need of my assistance. Her sickness came and went in waves of increasing violence that filled me with a sense of helpless dread. I tried to remember what I might have read about mushroom poisoning, but I could remember only that it was swift and violent, and often fatal.

I did remember, during one of Pam's brief periods of quiet, to get the telephone number of Laura May Hollis from Mrs. Maywood. I thought Mrs. Hollis ought to be warned, and that perhaps there was something preventive that she could do or take. I was too late for that, however. Nellie informed me that her mother had taken sick shortly after they had arrived home, but that her condition did not seem to be violent. If, as I suspected, the sickness sprang from the mushrooms on Pam's plate, Mrs. Hollis had taken only a single bite, and Nellie and I had been spared even that.

Doctor Williams, a kindly-looking old gentleman, finally arrived and took charge. I was more than happy to turn my patient over to him, and I found my way down to the kitchen. Heedless of Mrs. Maywood's disapproval, I made myself a pot of coffee and was seated on a stool drinking a cup when Mrs. Maywood and the doctor found me.

'That looks good,' he said. 'Mind if I have some with you?'

'Please do. How are the patients, Doctor?'

'Better. Both resting at the moment. They'll be all right, but they'll want a few days in bed, I venture to say. And see that they continue to drink that milk thistle;

that will do as well as anything.'

'What was it, anyway?'

He pulled out a chair to sit at the table. 'Oh, mushrooms, no doubt of it.

'That's impossible,' Mrs. Maywood said. 'Miss May Ellen picked them herself, and I cooked them. We'd both of us spotted them if there'd been any bad ones in the bunch.'

'I'm running some tests. But I'm as sure as sure can be, that's what it was.'

'Why, them poisonous things don't even look like sponges, not at all,' Mrs. Maywood insisted, her voice rising. She put her hands on her hips and gave him a withering look. 'I don't mind what it appears to be, that wasn't no mushroom poisoning. More than likely, something wrong with the steaks. One of them did smell a little ripe, now that I recollect.'

'We'll see.' the doctor sipped his coffee. 'I'll admit, it makes no sense how someone as knowledgeable as Mrs. Andrews could make that mistake, not to mention you cutting them up and cooking them without seeing the bad ones in the bunch, but I'll eat my hat if it doesn't turn out that's what it was.'

Mrs. Maywood gave a disdainful snort through her nostrils and went to the sink, where she began to wash out the towels she had brought downstairs with her.

The doctor turned his attention to me. 'I understand you and your sister helped pick the mushrooms.'

'Yes, and it's entirely possible I might have picked the wrong thing. I know nothing about them. I doubt Pam would have made a mistake, though. She seemed quite familiar with the various varieties.'

'It's hard to go wrong picking sponges. They're all safe, and they all look like sponges. And the poisonous ones all look like the traditional picture you have of a mushroom or a toadstool — some of them different in color, some of them broader or flatter, or different on the bellies, and some of them look like a hooded monk. But none of them look anything like a sponge.'

'I wish I could help,' I said, spreading my hands helplessly. 'I really don't remember anything out of the ordinary. They all looked the same to me.'

'Well, I'll let everyone know what the tests show. Although I doubt she'll believe it.'

'I'll tell you what she'll believe,' Mrs. Maywood said. 'The same as I believe. That was a Melungeon trick.'

'Now, Sadie,' the doctor began, but the housekeeper fixed her dark, angry eyes on me.

'A Melungeon trick, such as is done by people named Collins.'

I leapt to my feet, shocked by her words. 'But, you can't be serious. Pam is my own sister.'

'Her name ain't Collins.'

'It's true,' I told Doctor Williams, 'We're only half sisters, but still . . . '

'If I was you, Sadie Maywood,' he said, 'I'd hold my tongue. You could be getting yourself into a heap of trouble, making accusations like that.'

'I says what I thinks.' She lowered her eyes and turned back to the sink. 'I better take some fresh towels upstairs.' She strode out of the kitchen, almost knocking over Annie.

'Thank you for coming to my defense,'

I told the doctor.

'Don't you pay any mind to talk about Melungeons.'

Annie let drop the dishes that she was carrying.

'Melungeons,' she said in a throaty whisper, her dull eyes wide with fright. 'I know'd it.'

The doctor rolled his own eyes heavenward and said, 'I'd better be going.'

I saw him to the door. By the time I came back, Annie was on her knees, cleaning up the pieces of broken china.

'Now, Annie,' I said, as firmly as I was able, 'I want you to forget all this talk about Melungeons and such. Mrs. Andrews and my sister are the unfortunate victims of mushroom poisoning. The doctor assures me that's what it was.'

'It was bad spirits.'

'It was bad mushrooms.'

'There's curses on this house. It's just like those other things that happened.'

The silence stirred between us, like dust in a gust of wind, and then settled slowly down again.

'What other things?'

'That time your sister fell down the stairs. And that fire when there wasn't anybody around.'

I couldn't think what to say. I stared back into the girl's wide eyes and my mind raced backward over the time since I had arrived. I'd had an impression of something amiss, something Pam had been on the verge of telling me, and had kept to herself instead.

I heard Mrs. Maywood's footsteps on the stairs, coming down. I put a hand on the servant girl's arm. 'Annie, I'm sure there are no evil spirits here,' I said, although my voice sounded less than convincing even to me. 'You mustn't be frightened.'

'There's a devil's dance out there in the yard. That's a sure sign of a curse. They don't come around a blessed house.'

I had no time to reply before Mrs. Maywood came in. She looked from one to the other of us, and I had a strange feeling of guilt, as if I had been caught out in something I should not be doing. It was Annie, however, who bore the brunt of the housekeeper's displeasure.

'You've broken one of the good cups. If you aren't the clumsiest creature alive, I don't know who is. I've a mind to box your ears for you.'

She gave me a look that said she wasn't far from boxing mine, either. I hesitated, wondering if she would actually resort to beating the poor dimwitted girl before me, but I had the impression that Mrs. Maywood was more bark than bite.

As I went out, I said to Annie: 'If you get frightened, just come to me, all right?'

But she was already frightened, and so was Mrs. Andrews — and, I realized now, so was Pam.

Well, Pam I could deal with. In the morning, when she was better, I would have the truth out of her.

*   *   *

I spent the night in Pam's room, wanting to be close at hand despite the good doctor's assurance that she would need very little attention before morning. Pam was still sleeping when I rose in the morning; but when I returned a while later, having freshened myself and had a hasty cup of coffee in the kitchen, she was awake. 'How do you feel?'

'Only half as bad as I look.' She was weak and needed help to sit up. I fluffed up the pillows and put them behind her before pouring her a cup of coffee.

'You look fine. The doctor says after a day or two in bed you'll be fit as a fiddle.'

'What did he think the trouble was?'

'Mushrooms,' I said, and I went on to tell her of the argument with Mrs. Maywood on the subject.

Pam frowned darkly. 'I would have sided with Mrs. Maywood,' she said, sipping her coffee. 'I could have sworn in a court of law that the mushrooms we brought home were all perfectly safe.'

'But they plainly can't have been. Unless someone slipped some bad ones in when Mrs. Maywood wasn't looking.'

'It's not impossible.'

'But highly improbable. Who, for instance? There's no one here but us and Mrs. Andrews and Mrs. Maywood, and Annie — and frankly, that seems beyond her capabilities. Aside from the dogs, there hasn't been anyone else around since I've been here.'

That wasn't exactly true, though. There had been that mysterious young man hanging about, for no reason that I could fathom.

'Anyway, that would immediately raise the question, why? I'll grant that Mrs. Hollis and her daughter seem to have a competitive attitude toward Mrs. Andrews, but not that competitive, surely. Anyway, it was obviously your lunch that was bad, and if Mrs. Hollis and Mrs. Andrews hadn't had that silly quarrel, neither of them would have tasted your mushrooms and been harmed at all. And since Mrs. Andrews did get poisoned, too, she certainly wasn't trying to do you in. And while I don't think Mrs. Maywood is fond of you, I don't fancy her trying to murder you, which leaves us with no one but Annie — and you've got to admit, she's an unlikely candidate.'

'Still, I was certainly poisoned, that I can swear to.'

'Of course,' I said in a casual way, 'it

could be just like those other accidents, the ones you haven't told me about.'

Her eyes flew wide open. 'So you know about them?'

'Annie made mention of them, but I think you ought to tell me more fully.'

She sighed and put her cup aside. 'Chris, dear, I didn't tell you about them before because . . . well, after I thought about them, I really couldn't make up my mind to take them seriously. To begin with, there was a loose patch of carpeting on the stairs, and I tripped. Nothing happened, truly. I caught myself on the banister and all I suffered was a mildly sprained ankle, not even enough to keep me off it for more than a day.'

'But it might have been worse.'

'Yes. I might have been badly hurt. Or if someone less agile — someone like Mrs. Andrews, say — had tripped, it could have been really bad. And then just a day before you arrived, there was a fire in the room adjoining Mrs. Andrews's. No one knows how it started, although if you want my opinion, someone was smoking a cigarette when she shouldn't have been, and when she was called, she threw a still-smoldering stub into the wastebasket. Annie, for instance, does smoke, and she is careless.

'What I'm saying is, they were the sorts of accidents that could happen anywhere, particularly in a house as big and old as this one, and as carelessly managed. But to Mrs. Andrews's mind, it's a clear and present attempt by the Melungeons, presumably in spirit form, to finish off the Andrews clan. And unfortunately, this poisoning will be another. That's why I signed my letter the way I did.

'Then, afterward, I realized I was being silly. I was letting Mrs. Andrews's foolish belief in these bogeymen to make a believer out of me. That's why I didn't tell you when you first arrived. I was afraid you might believe with Mrs. Andrews that something dark and mysterious was going on.'

'But, Pam, something is wrong here. Three accidents so soon after one another, and no clear explanation of how they happened?'

'Melungeons?' She cocked an eyebrow.

'No, my sweet sister, I'll have you hatching no evil spirits in that dream-stuffed head of yours. I'll tell you what happened: one of us picked a bad mushroom without noticing, and it got into the food on my plate. Mrs. Andrews has been gathering those mushrooms all her life, and I thought I knew them pretty well, but perhaps there is a poisonous species that *does* look like the morels, and we were both just ignorant of that fact. As for those other accidents, they were just that — accidents. And if you even start with ghosts and hobgoblins and such, I will personally get out of this bed and begin packing your bags for you.'

I laughed and said, 'All right, have it your way.'

★ ★ ★

When I was away from her later, however, and carrying her tray downstairs, I found myself feeling differently again. I had meant to ask Pam if, in the legends, the devil's dance on the lawn was a bad omen, but I knew she would only scold me.

There was something amiss here in this house, something in the very atmosphere itself, as if it had permeated all this old wood, the way odors sometimes do. Accident? Human mischief? Or evil spirits? The latter certainly seemed farfetched. If they were accidents — three in a row — the coincidence was a bit thick; and as for human mischief, who could be the perpetrator?

Nor did a visit with Mrs. Andrews, who was also convalescing well, do anything to ease my fears. Although Mrs. Andrews was polite and even apologized that my visit should be marred, I thought I detected a certain reserve toward me. Or was I only imagining it?

'I know,' she said flatly, 'that we picked nothing but sponges yesterday. I had an eye on you girls all the time, knowing that you were amateurs, so to speak. No, there was no accident there.'

'But what do you think happened, then?'

She lowered her eyes and was silent for

a moment. When she did speak, it was more to herself than to me. 'They'll see us all dead and buried. They'll not rest until then.'

After a while I saw that she had drifted to sleep. I got up and quietly left her.

Pam was asleep, too. I suddenly wanted to be out of this house. The sun outside was warm and golden. Here, with the scent of spring flowers and the buzzing of an occasional bee, I could forget the unpleasantness of the past twenty-four hours. I walked, following much the same path that Mrs. Andrews, Pam and I had walked yesterday.

It was not until I was actually in the woods, its peace descending about me like a mantle, that I remembered yesterday's snake. I paused, thinking perhaps I ought to return to the house, but Mrs. Andrews had assured me there was really very little danger from snakes. I armed myself with a long stick, which I kept before me, poking the path with it, and I went on.

I saw no snakes. If there were any on the path, they heard me coming and fled.

What I did see were flowers in abundance, and the flashing colors of birds on the wing — here a cardinal, there a bluejay, and everywhere the sparrows and wrens. The woods were perfumed with scents that were mysterious to me, and exotic. The earth beneath my feet was not only earth, but a thick, yielding carpet of leaves and grass and moss. Gentle fern fronds reached out to playfully tickle my ankles.

Enveloped in a sea of sense experiences such as these, I lost all comprehension of time. At length, becoming gradually aware that I had walked a considerable distance and was growing a bit tired, I stopped to sit on a fallen log.

A woodpecker set up a hammering in a tree overhead. A small dead branch, having held on for no one knew how long, parted from its parent tree and came crashing down. The trees seemed to shake themselves a bit and rustle their leaves in its wake, like a hen will ruffle her feathers. Then they settled back down again and the disturbance was forgotten. In the distance, a pack of dogs barked and yelped to one another.

I watched a worm crawling along the log on which I sat. An oriole swooped down, all orange and black, and perched on a nearby branch, his little button eyes darting to and fro. He eyed the worm, and then me, and went away to return a moment later. The worm inched his way further and further along the log. The bird went again and came back the third time; at last he thought the worm had gotten far enough away from me, and looked appetizing enough to be worth the risk. He swooped down toward us, and in a flash had the worm in his mouth and was gone.

The barking of the dogs rose in pitch. They were closer now, coming in my direction, and they seemed to have gotten the scent of something. There was an air of excitement in their noisy communication.

My thoughts had been so far from any idea of danger that the barking of the dogs held no significance for me. But now, as I rose to continue my walk, something that Pam had said came back to me. She had talked of the dangers of these woods, of snakes and bears — and packs of wild dogs.

I listened unhappily to the braying and barking of the dogs, coming unmistakably closer.

I began to walk. In fact, at that precise moment, I did not know where I was. I was of no mind, though, to stand quietly in one spot while that noisy bunch of dogs sniffed me out and found me.

It may have been foolishness on my part, but I could not help thinking that I was the scent they had found and were on the trail of. Certainly, they were excited about something, and coming swiftly after it, and it was in my direction.

I had a glimpse of a fence in the distance, up a hill. Once I was on the other side of that, I would surely be quite safe from any approaching dogs.

The barking became a din, and a moment after, there was a crashing in the underbrush behind me. The lead dog emerged from a thicket and, seeing me, froze. Close on his heels came the others, seven in all. They were a motley crew of every size and color. The leader was a fierce-looking beast, easily the size of a full-grown Collie, his eyes glittering threateningly as they stared at me, his lips curled back to reveal twin rows of shining teeth.

He growled deep down in his throat, took a cautious step forward, and the others edged after him.

'Good dogs,' I tried to say, but the words lodged in my throat and refused to come forth. I glanced over my shoulder. The fence was some thirty feet away from me still, the dogs less than that.

The lead dog snarled. He seemed to sense that I was no match for them. He moved closer, his ears back, his tail down. He crouched low as he came, as if at any second he would spring.

I thought of Pam's advice regarding bears — stand still and let them charge. But these were no bears, and I was no hero. With a strangled little cry, I whirled about and bolted for the fence.

6

Of course they were faster than I. With great barking and yapping they were after me, and upon me before I had half reached the fence. The leader leapt at me, nearly knocking me over.

I still held my walking stick. I had forgotten it, but now I struck out wildly with it, hitting the great beast in the jaw. He gave a yelp of pain and fell back for a moment. In that moment, I made the fence and was scrambling up it.

The other hounds from hell followed their leader. When he fell away, they too fell away. Now, however, he seized his courage and came at me again, the others close in his wake. He caught my foot. I felt those awful teeth tear the flesh even through the leather of my shoe. I gave a frantic kick, freeing my foot, and threw myself over the top of the fence. I landed in a heap on the opposite side. The hounds jumped at the fence, making a terrible ruckus.

I lay for a moment, dazed and breathless. I had landed on one arm, and it had begun to send little tentative vibrations of pain up into my shoulder. I moved it, and found that fortunately it was not broken.

I sat up then, brushing myself off, and looked at the dogs, their wild faces made wilder still by their rage and frustration. They looked as if they would happily tear me limb from limb, if they could only get hold of me.

It suddenly looked as if they were going to get their opportunity. One of the dogs, running along the fence with his nose to the ground, discovered what I, in my terror, had not seen: a tear in the fence a few yards along. The cry went up, and the others rushed to where he was already wriggling under the fence.

I gave a low moan of horror and, scrambling to my feet, began to run. A tree stood only a few feet away, and I thought if I could climb that, the dogs could not follow.

Behind me, the dog in the lead had

made it through the fence. He gave a yelp of triumph and raced toward me.

I reached the tree, grabbing frantically at a branch to pull myself up, trying to dig my toes into the trunk. I got no more than a foot or so off the ground before the branch broke, sending me tumbling onto the ground again. I thought I heard a shout, and as I rolled onto my back, I had a vision of a great dog leaping over me. I screamed and closed my eyes, throwing my arms up to protect my face.

But the dogs did not attack. I heard barking and snarling and growling, but no razor-sharp teeth sank into my trembling flesh.

At last, I willed my eyes open. The first thing I saw was yet another dog, a brown-and-white spotted one easily as large as any of those in the pack, and quite obviously their match in courage, for he had leapt over me, putting himself between me and them, and he now held them at bay, barking and snarling. Once the leader of the pack tried to circle around him to get to me, but the big dog leapt toward him, teeth bared, and the leader rejoined his pack, growling in frustration, but without quite the courage to take on this challenger.

I saw all this in a second or two. Before I could even comprehend it, a twig snapped behind me and I jerked my head around to see a man running toward me. It was my spirit of the woods, the young man I had met before.

The wild pack had decided that two humans and another dog were more than they wanted to take on. They began to back away, yapping and growling. The young man went past me, charging threateningly toward them and yelling 'Git!' They slid away from his path, the group breaking and reforming a distance away. He stopped, bending down to pick up a stone, which he threw. It caught the lead dog on the rump, making him yelp, and he disappeared into the thicket with the others close behind.

I gave a long sigh of relief and sat up, rubbing myself gingerly. My rescuer, his dog at his side, came back to where I was sitting and knelt down. 'You all right?' he asked.

'Yes, thank you. You don't know how glad I am to see you.' I started to get up, but the sore arm gave me some trouble. At once my companion's arm went about me to help me stand. He left it there when I was on my feet, and I could not help but notice that it seemed ideally designed to fit where it was.

'Usually those varmints don't chase a human. You must have let them see you were scared. It got them all worked up.'

I said, a bit dryly, as I was still shaken by the incident, 'When I next see them, I'll apologize for upsetting them.'

'You're shaking like a leaf. Come on, sit down over here till you get yourself back together.'

He helped me to a fallen tree, seating me on it, and stood with one foot propped up on the log. I took a moment to examine my arm, which was only bruised a bit, and to check another bruise on one leg. He waited silently and, when I looked up, he was watching me with the half-smile that I remembered from our previous meetings. The sun was behind him, giving his dark hair a halo entirely at odds with his devilish grin.

'I suppose we ought to introduce ourselves, if we're going to keep meeting like this,' I said, holding out a hand. 'I'm Chris Collins. Christine Collins, but everybody calls me Chris.'

'Gabriel Goins. Everyone calls me Gabe. Pleased to meet you.'

'Gabriel,' I said, thinking aloud. 'An archangel. That's a sort of a spirit.'

'Beg pardon?'

'Nothing.' I smiled up at him and said, as one would to a child, 'I'm from New York City. Do you know where that is?'

'I've heard tell of it.' His drawl seemed to thicken.

'It's a long way from here. I suppose you've lived here all your life?'

He nodded, looking sober and duly impressed by my New York background. I supposed that it represented to him, as it must to millions of country folk, the 'big city.'

'Most of it.'

The conversation faltered. After a moment I asked, 'And did you go to school?' I had a vague idea that a school education was not so common in these parts.

'Oh, yes. I'm still going,' he said, grinning again.

I had a terrible vision of this strapping young woodsman, who must be twenty-three or twenty-four years old, and well over six feet tall, in a one-room school with a group of children of assorted ages, struggling to master his three r's. 'And what grade are you in now?'

'Well . . . ' He paused thoughtfully. 'I got my bachelor's last year from Columbia University. That's in New York City. And I'm working on my master's now, in history.'

The drawl had vanished altogether, and that country simpleton grin he had been affecting was replaced by the earlier, very mischievous smile.

My face went crimson. I could feel the red rushing up through it. I got up with what few shreds of dignity I could manage and, brushing myself off, said, 'How nice for you. Now if you'll excuse me, I really should be going.'

'Wait,' he said.

'So that you can have some more fun at my expense? No, thank you.' I walked hurriedly, but he easily caught up with me and grabbed my arm, making me stop. I was humiliated and furious. 'Let me go,' I demanded.

'All right. But these hills are dangerous if you don't know them. You'd better let me take you back home.'

'I can get there by myself, thank you.'

'Not in that direction. The Andrews place is back the other way.'

I stopped again, wishing the ground would simply swallow me up. Of course he was grinning again, and even I had to see how stupidly I was behaving. I let some of the stiffness go out of my shoulder and tried a humble smile.

'I'm sorry. Truly. I treated you as if you were some country lout, and I deserved what I got. Will you forgive me?'

'It's I who should apologize. I didn't mean to offend you, but how do you go about telling someone that you're not as dumb as they think?'

'Do you really have your degree? He nodded. 'Columbia?'

'In New York City. It's a long way from here.'

I giggled. I couldn't help it. I just saw how funny I must have sounded to him, not to say pretentious. When he saw that I was no longer angry, he too began to chuckle. The dog, the big spotted brute who had come to my rescue, lay down on the ground, watching us with more than a little puzzlement.

'Well,' I said when the laughter had died down, 'I suppose I should let you escort me home. I think I've had all the thrills I need for one day. An encounter with a snake would just about do me in.'

'It isn't snakes so much that you've got to worry about here. Have you got any idea where you are?'

'Not the slightest. I was just wandering, and then when the dogs came along, I ran without thinking.'

'This is called Hungry Hill. Even the local people try to avoid coming up here.'

'But why? It's quite lovely, and surely the dogs aren't a usual threat?'

'Watch.' He picked up a large rock. I don't know what it must have weighed, but I could see that it was heavy from the way his muscles bulged as he lifted it over his head. Lift it he did, though, and with a grunt he threw it. It came to the ground some ten feet in front of him — and at once, rock and ground both disappeared with a clatter.

'What on earth?' I gasped.

'That's why they call it Hungry Hill. It can swallow a man up like that, just as easily as it swallowed that rock.' He took my hand and led me closer to where the rock had disappeared. 'Sinkholes. They're common to most of this part of the country. The roof of an underground cave collapses, or wears thin enough to give under a man's weight. Usually the opening is obvious, and the danger minimal. But sometimes the visible opening is very small, or gets covered up with leaves and twigs and such, so that you can step into it without even seeing it, and suddenly you've disappeared into the earth. They can go down hundreds of feet. Hungry Hill is honeycombed with sinkholes. The whole heart of the hill is a chain of underground caves where the surface above has worn thin. Look, there's a hole there, and another one just over here.'

He pointed and, following his finger, I saw two large openings in the earth. These two were visible enough for me to have avoided stepping into them, but the spot where he had thrown the rock had looked quite ordinary and safe. I could very easily have stepped upon it and fallen through in an instant, perhaps never to be seen again. I shuddered involuntarily. 'And I might have wandered into here without knowing. No one told me.'

'The locals just plain forget. They've lived with it all their lives, and they take it for granted, and they mostly avoid the hill. And your sister probably didn't even know. Come on, as long as I'm showing you things you might as well see this too.'

He took my hand again and led me up the hill. 'Is it safe?' I asked, looking at the ground beneath my feet, which I expected to fall away at any moment.

'You're with me.'

He said it matter-of-factly, but I had an

immediate impression that the implication in his words was quite true. He looked like a man with whom a woman was safe, and at once my fears fell away, to be replaced by a confident trust.

We had come to a path and we followed it uphill around a low, overhanging bluff. We came over a rise and the ground swooped downward before us. A natural basin had formed here and there was a pond at our feet, but this was not the sort of pond one thinks of in lovely pastoral settings, with wild ducks skimming its surface and fish shimmering beneath. I saw at a glance that there was something ugly and obscene about this place. The water was black and had an eerie green iridescence. Even the mud at its edges was not merely mud, but a repulsive black slime that was unspeakably disgusting.

'How awful,' I said, instinctively drawing close into the circle of the arm he had once again put about me. 'What is it?'

'Devil's Pond. The hill folk say he comes here to swim.'

'I can well believe it.'

'What it really is, is another sinkhole. This one was probably over an underground stream to begin with, and when the roof collapsed it became a lake of mud down there. It was in a natural basin, too, so that it caught all the water and running mud from the hill, and over the years, centuries, probably, it filled with mud until it had formed the black lake. It's like quicksand in there. If a man walked into it, he could be trapped in that ooze, unable to free himself.'

'And to think, because of my wounded pride, I might have marched away from you and right up here.'

'You'd have seen it first. Anyway, I was prepared to fling you over my shoulder if I had to and carry you home.'

I looked up into his handsome face. 'And you know, I think you would have done just that.'

'Oh, yes. Us country boys are pretty crude at times.'

We stood like that for a moment. His arm was still about me, feeling incredibly strong and comforting. Something quickened inside me. There was a strange sense of inevitability about the moment, as if my entire life had been building upward to this, its highest point.

I sensed a change in his attitude toward me. His moods changed with mercurial swiftness. 'I'll take you home now,' he said gruffly.

I nodded mutely, and we began to descend the hill. I tried not to think of what was singing in my heart. He was not at all what I had wanted, what I had told myself repeatedly I was waiting for. I wanted a suave, polished man, a somewhat rugged version of Prince Charming. This man I was walking alongside was not at all like that. I had never seen him in anything but jeans and an open shirt, and his taste in beverages probably ranged from elder-berry wine to corn whiskey. He was very handsome, that was true, but not by any stretch of the imagination suave or polished.

And yet . . . and yet . . . he took my hand to help me over a little stream, and my heartbeat quickened, and I could not meet his eyes because I was afraid I would see in them something less than what I wanted.

Of course, it was inevitable. I had been walking around most of my life with stars in my eyes. If ever anyone had been ripe to fall in love, it was I.

Then I had come here, into this strange milieu, with its unsettling atmosphere. There was, moreover, the fact that I had just been scared half out of my wits by a pack of wild dogs, and this woods spirit beside me had been the one to rescue me.

Of course, I would not take it seriously. He had given me no indication at all that the attraction was mutual. He had found me amusing, and he had been ordinarily friendly, but it plainly went no further than that, for which I was grateful.

And yet . . .

We had come to the fence bordering the Andrews' garden. He helped me over it. When I was on the other side, he said, 'I'll leave you here.'

'Must you? I wish you'd come in and have something to drink. Do you know my sister, Pam?'

'I know who she is. We've never met.'

He smiled in that mysterious way of his. 'I know most everything that goes on here.'

I thought again of my early impressions of him — the notion that he was not quite human, but a spirit, haunting this house. It was a role to which he seemed well suited, and I could still easily imagine him in it.

'Does this place have such a fascination for you, then?'

Was it only my imagination, or was his smile just a little bitter? Was there something cynical in the way he replied, 'It does, yes'?

Our conversation was interrupted by a loud cry from behind me. Startled, I turned and looked in the direction of the house. There, to my further surprise, was Mrs. Andrews. She had evidently just come from her bed. She wore a nightgown over which she had hastily donned a robe. Her hair was still covered by a cap, and on her feet were a pair of slippers.

Seeing Mrs. Andrews like this would have been quite enough of a shock, but that was not all. At her side was Jed, the hired man, and he was bearing a big, antiquated-looking rifle. The two of them stopped a few yards from us and, to my horror, the hired man raised the gun so that it was pointed at us.

'Stand right there,' Mrs. Andrews barked.

'Mrs. Andrews, what on earth?' I stammered.

'Get away from him, Miss Collins. You, Goins, you stay right where you are. If he moves to cross that fence, Jed, you shoot him.'

7

I was so astonished that I could scarcely speak nor move. I stared wide-eyed at the pair confronting us — the old woman, pale as a ghost with her recent illness, her eyes wild and feverish-looking, and the gaunt hired man, whose face was quite expressionless, but who trained the gun steadily on us.

'It's a good thing I looked out my window and saw you coming,' Mrs. Andrews said. 'Why, I'd bet anything you'd have come right on up to the house. Get away from him, I say, Miss Collins. He can't hurt you now.'

'I can hardly think he would, Mrs. Andrews, I must ask some explanation for this outrageous behavior.'

'Move away,' she insisted.

'I will not. Or would you have Jed shoot me as well?'

I saw some of her fiery determination fade. Perhaps she saw that I was angry and likely to be just as stubborn as she. Indeed, I would have allowed myself to be shot before I would have moved from that spot at her command. I was shamed and furious that Gabe, who had rescued me and escorted me home, should have been welcomed so rudely.

It was Gabe who resolved this confrontation. 'I'd best be going,' he said softly. Our eyes met. He was smiling, quite cynically now, and I could see that whatever bravado he might assume, he was hurt by this treatment — as indeed, any sensible person would be.

That hurt made him suddenly utterly real to me, something more than a spirit or a simple country man. 'Where will I find you?'

His grin widened. 'Where do devils live? On the wind, in the trees?' His eyes teased me but he grew quickly sober. 'The spot on the road where we first met. There's a path there that cuts around the edge of the woods, over a creek, and right to where I live — when you come to another road, a dirt one, go to the right. Our name is on the mailbox. And bring old Zeke with you. He knows the way, and he ain't afraid of me. Besides, he'll keep you out of trouble.'

'Gabe Goins, you devil!' Mrs. Andrews shouted. 'Are you gonna git, or do I have to shoot your head off?'

He looked past me with a mocking smile. 'My dear lady, if you shot my head off, you'd only have me haunting you in headless form, and that wouldn't be very pleasant, would it?'

She gasped and clutched at her robe, holding it closed over her heaving bosom. I think if she had held the gun herself, she might have shot him then, so violent was her reaction to him.

With a quick nod at me he was gone, striding away up the hill, his back straight and proud. If he remembered there was a gun following him, he gave no evidence of it.

I had not forgotten, however. I watched him until he was out of sight among the trees. Then I whirled about and marched to where Mrs. Andrews and Jed stood. 'How dare you?' I demanded, too angry to think of manners or respect for her age.

The strength of my anger plainly did not intimidate her, however. 'You are a fool. Don't you know what that man is? Man? Ha! He isn't a man at all, he's a devil!'

'I know that he saved my life.'

'He'd like to take mine. Mine and my son's, and, yes, your sister's, too.'

I saw, out of the corner of my eye as it were, Mrs. Maywood rushing toward us across the lawn, looking alarmed. As it was, she was coming none too soon, and she had cause to be alarmed. Mrs. Andrews had literally sprung from her sickbed to rush down here and confront Gabe and me. The violence of her feelings had given her the strength to do so, but even now as she and I quarreled, that flame began to burn out. I saw the fire in her eyes grow dull, and she swayed unsteadily.

'Mrs. Andrews,' I began, but the force had gone out of my words. I was not a hard enough person to quarrel with an old woman who was ill, regardless of how abominably she had just behaved. And she was ill, certainly. Her eyes rolled upward and I saw she was going to faint. I sprang toward her but Jed, who was much faster than he looked, had his arm about her in a flash; and in another, Mrs. Maywood was there as well, supporting the old woman from the other side. I was excluded, made an outsider; and although I knew that she had been in the wrong, I felt a pang of guilt. I ought perhaps to have been a little gentler with her, knowing that she was not well.

'Now you've done it,' Mrs. Maywood said, shaking her head angrily at me. 'I suppose it will please you to kill the old woman this way.'

'But what did I do?'

I demanded of deaf ears, though, for the two hired people ignored me. Mrs. Andrews had sunk into unconsciousness, so that Jed had to pick her up in his arms and carry her back to the house, Mrs. Maywood hurrying alongside.

I was left alone by the fence. I had no idea why Mrs. Andrews should have reacted so violently to the sight of Gabe Goins escorting me home. That there was some quarrel between them was evident, for beneath his cynicism and his considerably better manners, I had detected a dislike for her no less real, if less violent, than hers for him. I somehow felt myself caught between these two, just as I had been a few minutes before when they had confronted one another.

Pam was on the phone when I came in. 'Yes, darling,' she said, and I knew she was talking to Peter. 'No, there's no need for you to rush back. It was nothing more than a bit of something tainted, and upset tummies. No, it wouldn't be practical for you to come back now.'

I personally would not want a man to be practical when I wasn't feeling well, but he was her fiancé, I thought, not mine, and I kept that thought to myself.

When she had hung up the phone, I told her what had happened. She looked appropriately alarmed when I told her of the wild dog pack, and relieved and puzzled when I told her of the rescue by my handsome woods spirit.

'But who can he be?' she mused. 'I

haven't met anyone like that since I've been here.'

'His name is Goins, Gabriel Goins. To tell you the truth, I met him before, when I first came. I stopped along the road to ask him for directions.'

She laughed lightly and said, 'Goins. That explains why I haven't met him. It's a Melungeon name. And around this house, a particularly disliked one. The Goins have been bitter enemies of the Andrews since those first quarrels in the early settlement days. Much of this land, so the story goes, belonged to the Goins before the Andrews usurped it. Of all the Melungeons, Mrs. Andrews hates and fears that family the most.'

'Then that explains it. He brought me home and Mrs. Andrews saw us from her window and came to meet us with a gun.'

'My dear Chris, you do stir things up, don't you? You might as well have brought that pack of dogs into the house as Gabe Goins; it would have caused less trouble.' She studied my face for a moment. 'And now you're thinking perhaps you ought to leave.'

'It was a hateful thing to do. But she has been sick, and fear has been gnawing at her for a long time, I think. I can't believe she's ordinarily as mean and vicious as she was today.'

'She isn't, truly. I suppose when she's recovered, she'll feel terrible about quarreling with you, and want to apologize.'

'She's so sure she's haunted by the Melungeons. It's hard to blame her for what she does.'

There was a knock at the door just then, and Annie came in to say that Mrs. Andrews wanted to see me.

I found Mrs. Andrews once again in bed, and Mrs. Maywood fussing over her.

'I suppose you've come to cause more trouble,' the housekeeper said.

'Annie said you wanted to see me,' I said to Mrs. Andrews, choosing not to argue with Mrs. Maywood.

'Yes,' Mrs. Andrews said. 'Sadie, leave us alone.'

'You need someone to look after you,' Mrs. Maywood said.

'Nonsense. Miss Collins is not going to

try to throttle me, although she might well wish to.'

Mrs. Maywood went out, muttering under her breath. When we were alone, Mrs. Andrews said, 'You mustn't mind Sadie.'

'I can't help but admire her loyalty to you.'

'That is gracious of you. You should have been born a southern girl, I think.' She smiled benignly upon me. It was difficult to think that this was the same woman who, less than an hour before, had threatened Gabe with a rifle and screamed angrily at me.

She seemed to follow my thought. 'You must forgive me for causing you embarrassment. You are a guest here, and I ought to have been more courteous to you.' She emphasized the last two words slightly. I thought she was pointing out that her apology was for me only, and did not apply to her treatment of Gabe.

'I am sure Mr. Goins was far more embarrassed than I.'

'Him? That I don't regret, I must tell you. I would rather shoot one of them than permit them on the property.'

'Isn't that a little strong?'

'Is it? I tell you, they long to see me dead. They're devils, the lot of them.'

'I can't believe Gabe feels so toward you.'

'Doesn't he? You think I'm a crazy old woman. Go to that dresser, the upper right hand drawer. Go on. Open it. There's a letter under those gloves.'

I found the letter and brought it back to her. She tore it from its envelope, scanning the sheet of yellowed paper within.

'Let me just find the part. You think I'm wicked. Well, I tried once to set things right with the Melungeons. When my husband died, and running this place fell to me, I thought I ought to set those old quarrels right, and since it was with the Goins that we'd mostly fought, I wrote to old man Goins to suggest we air our differences. Ah, here it is.' She held the letter toward me. 'Just read that paragraph — that one right there.'

The paragraph she had indicated was in a rough scrawl that ran at a slant across the paper. 'I got just one wish,' it read, 'and that is to see every Andrews in the county dead and buried. And I hope it's by my hand.'

'It was your Gabe's father who wrote that. Now do you see why I daren't let them on the property?'

'But, his father . . . I don't think Gabe could feel like that.'

'Not share his father's feelings? Don't be a fool.' And although it was rude of her, I could see her point. Gabe might have inherited his father's hatred. And as to that, I had seen by the look in his eyes that there was a strong feeling on his part regarding this house, and Mrs. Andrews herself. Why else would he hang about as he had been doing when I saw him? And hadn't there been a strong bitterness when he had parted from me by the fence, a bitterness undeniably directed toward Mrs. Andrews?

I handed the letter back to her. My heart told me that Gabe could not be like that, but Mrs. Andrews thought otherwise.

'No, as long as I am mistress here, there won't be any Melungeons in this house, nor on the property, and most certainly no one by the name of Goins,' she said in a voice that brooked no argument. 'And now, I think I must sleep. I'm very tired, but I want you to stay on as long as you like, and I want you not to be angry with me for speaking so strongly. It's for the best, believe me, dear.'

I told her I was not angry and that I would stay. Even had she not aroused my sympathy, I would have felt it best for me to stay while Pam recovered from her illness, and I could not but feel sorry for the old woman in the bed, her eyes already closing with exhaustion.

I came from her room to find Annie coming along the hall toward me. 'There's a telephone call for you,' she said.

I followed her down to the parlor where the phone was. I could not imagine who would be calling me here, since hardly anyone else knew where I was.

It was Doctor Williams. 'My wife and I thought you might want to come for supper,' he said when we had exchanged greetings.

I was genuinely flattered that he should trouble to think of me, and told him so. 'But I think I ought to stay here with Pam.'

Pam, however, when I told her of it, thought differently. 'Don't be a goose,' she said. 'The most I'm going to do is have a tray in my room, and probably snooze. All you'll accomplish here is to keep me awake when I want to sleep. And Mrs. Maywood would probably just as soon you'd go. Besides, it will do you good.'

In the end, she persuaded me to call Doctor Williams back and ask if the invitation was still open. He told me that it was, and we arranged that I should be there at six.

I left Home Acres at five. It was only a short drive to the doctor's house, but I planned also to pay a brief visit on the Hollises, to see how Mrs. Hollis was recuperating.

Nellie greeted me, making me most welcome. She was a not unattractive girl, although like her mother she had an air of artificiality that made it difficult for one to care very deeply about her. Mrs. Hollis, who had been stricken less seriously than Pam and Mrs. Andrews, was seated on the terrace behind their house. The afternoon was waning and the air, so warm just a short time before, had a damp coolness to it.

'So nice of you to come,' Mrs. Hollis purred, 'although I'm feeling much better now. Doctor Williams says I should be tiptop in another couple of days. You'll have some wine, of course? You'll like mine after that nasty stuff May Ellen serves.'

I drank a little glass of dandelion wine, which was a new experience for me. It was delicious and sweet, and I complimented her on it, while refraining from comparing it to what Mrs. Andrews had served.

'I hear you had some trouble over that Goins boy,' Mrs. Hollis said.

I must have looked very surprised, because she smiled and said, 'Annie, that kitchen girl, is all the time running over here to borrow things from my Nellie, and she manages to keep us informed.'

Since it was two miles or more from the Andrews' house to here, I wondered that Annie should be 'all the time running over here,' but the girl was simple-minded, and I had a feeling that she was more than a little encouraged to come by, so that Nellie and her mother could keep up on all the gossip.

Mrs. Hollis tried one or two times to pry tidbits of gossip from me, but I carefully avoided being led into that trap; and when I had finished my wine, I said that I must be going.

'I was hoping,' Mrs. Hollis said, 'that you'd stay for supper. We don't have a lot of servants, like some folks, but my Nellie is a very fine cook.' Nellie blushed modestly.

I explained that I should very much like to stay, but that I had already accepted an invitation to eat with Doctor Williams and his wife.

Mrs. Hollis's eyebrows went up. 'Oh, I see,' she said, like a hound that has caught an interesting scent. 'This, I suppose, is so you can meet the nephew.'

'Nephew?'

Mrs. Hollis nodded. 'Oh, yes indeed. Down visiting from Cincinnati. He's a doctor, as I understand, and quite well off, and such a charming young man. I only met him once, but he was very pleasant. And so handsome, wasn't he, Nellie?'

'Yes,' Nellie said, flushing slightly. I had the feeling she had taken quite an interest in this visiting doctor herself.

'And he's single,' Mrs. Hollis added, making that remark her *pièce de rèsistance*.

'If he's as handsome and charming as you say, and as well off, he probably won't be single for long.'

'He seemed mightily interested in my Nellie.' I suspected that her mind was already at work judging whether I represented a threat to her plans for the doctor and Nellie.

8

The doctor's house was a pleasant cottage, quite modest in comparison to the Andrews home, but comfortable and warming. Mrs. Williams met me cheerily at the door. 'You're Miss Collins,' she said. 'And I am the doctor's wife. Do come in, won't you? I'm so pleased to meet you.' She led me into a room crowded with massive chairs and drowned in walls of books. It was a man's room, comfortable and informal.

Doctor Williams rose from his chair to greet me. 'So glad you decided to come,' he said, steering me around a high wingback chair. 'This is my nephew, Phillip Arthur. Phil, this is Miss Collins.'

'Chris, please. How do you do?'

'Phil has come for a brief visit. I thought an evening of your company might brighten his stay. Oh, and vice versa, of course.'

I murmured something appropriate,

hardly aware of what. It was really quite astonishing to meet one's Prince Charming just as one has imagined him. He was tall, with light brown hair, and he was very good-looking. He was wearing tweeds, and just now at his side was the doctor's Irish setter. He looked every inch the country gentleman. *Now, why couldn't I have met you a few days sooner?* I thought.

A prince he truly was, too. He was highly personable and well-mannered. The four of us chatted easily, Mrs. Williams popping in and out to see to things in the kitchen, and I found Phil easy to talk with.

He seemed taken with me as well, and it would have been a romantic idyll, if only the image of Gabe Goins would not keep intruding itself upon my mind. I sorely wanted it to vanish. Gabe was not the man I wanted. I was sure of it. What had he to offer? No matter how much education he had, he would still be a country boy at heart, and not a country gentleman, either. These hills and woods were a part of him. If I were to marry him, I would more than likely find myself in some little shack far back in the hills, but to marry Phillip Arthur meant being the wife of a doctor in Cincinnati, where there were operas and symphonies and art museums and good restaurants.

And now, I thought, laughing inwardly at myself, *you have really gone bonkers.* Already I was comparing marriage with these two men, and neither one of them had expressed the slightest interest in marrying me. Certainly Gabe had not, and seemed unlikely ever to do so, and I had just met the doctor's nephew.

But I found myself thinking, if I *were* to marry Phil . . .

★   ★   ★

'It was the mushrooms, of course,' the doctor said. 'The tests were conclusive.'

'And yet,' I said, 'It's certainly strange how it happened. And that's not the only strange thing that's happened.' I went on to relate the other incidents that had occurred, including that angry confrontation between Gabe and Mrs. Andrews. I thought, although I might have been imagining it, that Phil was rather interested in how I came to meet Gabe and who he was in this narrative.

'There is certainly bad blood between the Goins and the Andrewses,' Doctor Williams said, 'although I had no idea how bad it was. Old Ned Goins is the kind of man to cling to a grudge.'

'It sounds like one of those old mountain feuds,' Phil said. 'The Hatfields and the McCoys.'

'As to those other things, they could all be accidents and coincidence,' Doctor Williams said.

'They could be,' I agreed, 'but Mrs. Andrews doesn't believe that. She believes that she is being haunted by Melungeons.'

'And you?' Phil said, looking steadily at me. 'What do you think?'

'I don't know what to think. I can't believe that the house is really haunted.'

'Still, you might be in some danger.'

Strange to say, I hadn't until now thought of myself as being in any danger

— and yet, there it was. If there was danger, it threatened everyone at Home Acres, didn't it?

Mrs. Williams rose from her chair with a little laugh. 'Heavens,' she said, 'you're making me afraid, and goodness knows what you're doing to poor Miss Collins, talking about danger and hauntings and the like. I'll tell you what I think. I think if you prescribed some nerve pills for Mrs. Andrews, all the ghosts and the hauntings would just vanish.'

We all laughed, and I for one could not with certainty dispute what she said. Mrs. Andrews was frightened, and fear can play tricks upon the mind. To change the subject, I turned my attention upon Phillip. 'Will you be here for long?'

'Leaves tomorrow,' Doctor Williams answered for him.

Mrs. Williams said, altogether too quickly, 'That isn't definite, of course.'

Phil smiled and said, 'I may stay on for a few days. I'm on vacation, and I have no firm plans.'

'Well, I thought you were going to drive on down to Miami and . . . oh.' Doctor

Williams seemed finally to grasp the significance of the change in plans. 'We're always happy to have you stay, of course, and I imagine Miss Collins would enjoy some company.'

'Will I see more of you?' Phil asked, looking directly into my eyes.

I lowered my lashes. 'I'm sure if you stay, we'll see one another.'

The rest of the evening was spent pleasantly. I had helped Mrs. Williams clear the table and we played a few hands of bridge. Phil chose me for a partner, and he was patient with my somewhat tentative playing. He himself played well. When we had finished two rubbers, we had won, more as a result of his well-thought-out game than from any contribution of mine.

'I think I should be going,' I said, when the game was ended. 'It's nearly ten, and frankly I've adopted the custom of early to bed, early to rise.' I thanked the doctor and his wife, who insisted I must come again, and Phil strolled with me to my car.

I put the window down and started up

the motor. 'May I call you?' he asked, leaning down to the window. He smiled, showing perfect white teeth.

'I hope you will.' We looked at each other for a long moment.

'Well, good night then,' he said, straightening up and stepping away from the car. I started down the long drive, and in the mirror I saw him turn and make his way up the steps to the front door.

I was not quite on the road when something moved off to the left, catching my eye. The moon broke through the clouds just at that moment, and I saw a man standing in the shadows by a tree, watching me.

It startled me so, I hardly knew what to think. I braked the car, thinking that he must want something. He had looked as if he were waiting, but when I rolled the window down again and leaned out to look back, there was no one there.

Had I only imagined it? Where had he gone, and why? He had seemed to be watching me, although that might have been nothing more than my imagination.

I hadn't really seen him clearly enough to recognize him, let alone know what he was doing.

I looked again. There was a thicket just past the trees. He could very easily have disappeared into that, and there were no doubt scores of perfectly good reasons why he should wish to do so. Probably he had no business being here on the doctor's property — and probably, it had nothing at all to do with me.

Something else occurred to me, though: I suddenly realized that it might not be the wisest thing for me to sit here with the car open and the window down, on this dark lane alone at night. My hand went to the door lock and, rolling up the window, I quickly started the car up again.

Had someone been there, or had I seen — what? Another spirit?

*   *   *

There was one thing that I must do, and I set out after an early lunch the next day to do it. I had to see Gabe to apologize to him for that dreadful scene with Mrs. Andrews.

I followed Gabe's instructions and went first to the kennel in back to free the hound, Zeke. He remembered me and greeted me with enthusiasm. His first inclination was to take the direct path into the woods, but when he saw that I meant to go by the road, he came along with me agreeably; and when we reached the lane, he took the lead. We walked that long lane between the cedars. At the road, Zeke waited patiently to see which direction I wanted to go before again taking the lead.

I found the path cutting off the road, just as Gabe had said. It followed around the edge of the wood, so that I rarely had that uneasy feeling of plunging into the thick of it. Zeke occasionally rushed off into the trees on some scent of his own, but he was never more than a minute or two away from me. He seemed utterly practiced in escorting city-bred girls through these country environs.

It was not an awfully long distance. I had walked no more than thirty minutes from the time I let Zeke out of his kennel until I came to the creek Gabe had mentioned. Stepping stones led across it in a neat row, and soon after I crossed it I came to the dirt road. I turned right as instructed and saw a house just a few yards along.

I confess I felt a sinking feeling as I approached the house. This was just the sort of place one envisioned when one thought of people in the Tennessee hills. The fence that had once surrounded it had fallen over except for one corner. The building itself, in fact, looked in danger of falling over. It was badly run down, and very much needed a coat of paint.

A pair of dogs came to greet us. They seemed to recognize Zeke and he, giving me a measuring look, decided that I had reached my destination and would not need his services for a few minutes. He bounded out of sight around the house with his friends.

Out of the corner of my eye, I saw a curtain move at one of the windows, so that I knew someone was watching as I came up the steps to the narrow front porch.

Despite the watcher at the window, there was a long wait before anyone answered my knock. I was about to knock again when the door finally opened, but no more than a crack. 'What do you want?' the woman in the opening asked.

'Is Gabe here?' I asked.

The old woman stared at me without answering. The silence became uncomfortable. It occurred to me that perhaps the woman, whom I could now see was not as old as I had first thought, was hard of hearing. I said, speaking louder and more distinctly, 'I'd like to see Gabe, if I may.'

A man's hand appeared on the door edge, swinging it open, and then the man himself was revealed, standing behind the woman. I knew at once that this must be Ned Goins, Gabe's father. He was a tall, strong man with the suggestion still of the good looks that had been passed on to Gabe, but it was more than the physical resemblance that identified him for me. This, I knew instinctively, was the man who had written that letter to Mrs. Andrews, the man Doctor Williams had spoken of as strong-willed and capable of all sorts of meanness. The eyes that were fixed on me were cold, filled with the threat of violence. I had never met the man — there could be nothing between us — and yet he looked at me with such cold loathing that I felt my skin crawl.

He said, 'You the girl's fixin' to marry the Andrews boy?'

I tried to smile, although my face felt stiff and unresponsive. 'That's my sister,' I said. 'I'm here for a visit.'

'That's just as bad.' He spat past me onto the floor of the porch.

I felt I had at least to make an effort to melt some of this unreasoning hostility. 'I'm sorry you feel that way,' I said. 'I would like . . . '

'Gabe ain't here,' he interrupted me, and with that the door slammed in my face.

I was speechless. I felt angry and humiliated, and I would have liked to kick that door off its hinges. I understood suddenly what it was like to be on the receiving end of unreasoning prejudice.

I became gradually aware of a distant hammering sound. Someone was driving nails into wood, not too far distant. I thought perhaps I might find Gabe, or at least someone a trifle more friendly who could tell me where he was. I followed the sound of the hammering, around the corner of the house.

I found Gabe repairing what I saw, as I came closer, was a henhouse. He was stripped to the waist, his skin gleaming in the sunlight as he lifted and held the pale-looking boards. He saw me come around the corner of the house and put aside his tools quickly, and put on his shirt. Zeke, who had been in the rear with his friends, came up with tail wagging in welcome, as if he had known all along I would not like what I found inside, and that I should have come along with him, where welcome was to be found.

Gabe looked pleased to see me. 'I've been away most of the last five years,' he said, indicating the henhouse. 'Things seem to have gotten into pretty bad shape.'

It was, I think, a roundabout way of

apologizing for the ramshackle appearance of the place. I realized that, being away so often, he could not have kept things up, and I could hardly hold him to blame if no one else had, either.

'There's just you and your parents?'

'I've got a sister, too, but she's doesn't live with us. She lived in Nashville for a while, went to a special school there, and now she's got a job where she lives, so she isn't here very often.'

'And you just got back yourself.' He had taken my arm and walked with me to where a plain wooden bench and a plank table sat in the shade of a beech tree.

'Just the day before you came.'

'It's odd; I can't seem to think of you away from here, away from these hills and the woods.'

'They're sure a part of me.' He looked around as if seeing things for the first time. 'I go, but I always come back. I always will.'

I thought that he emphasized his last words, as if he wanted to tell me something more than the surface statement conveyed. I felt my pulse quicken slightly.

149

I said, 'I came because I wanted to apologize for what happened yesterday.'

He grinned. 'I understand about that. It wasn't any fault of yours. Besides, if you've been to the house just now, I suspect you got just as poor a welcome.'

My face told him the truth, so that there was no need for me to reply. He glanced once toward the house and I saw a glint of something angry in his eyes. 'These people have been hating one another for years. Sometimes when I'm away from here, I think back on it and wonder if it could be as real and as violent as it is; but when I come home, it's still here, still just as bad.'

'But you don't feel like your father does, surely?'

'Don't I?' He kicked at the bare earth with the toe of his shoe. 'When I'm away, I think that I don't. I think I'm too smart and too well-educated for that. But whenever I come back . . . ' He let his voice trail off for a moment. 'Sometimes I go over and sit in that tree behind the Andrews house, and stare at the house for hours, and I hate the people in it, because they shouldn't be there — because that was all stolen from my family. And because of that, my family is poor and my mother old before her years, and I've had to work like a fool to get through school, even with scholarships.'

He stopped abruptly and was silent. I did not want to speak. I was, for the present, one of those people in that house. Yet I knew he did not hate me, although his family might; and perhaps through knowing me he could see that unreasoning hate for the self-harming delusion that it was, and could shed himself of it in time.

Zeke came to sit before me, eyeing me questioningly. I stood, thinking it best to keep this visit brief. Gabe rose too, and walked around the house with me.

'I'm sorry if my family was rude,' he said, when we had come to the dirt road.

'I understand how it is. But it doesn't have to remain like that, that's the important thing.'

'You're an optimist.'

'I think you may be too.'

I left him, hurrying with Zeke back the

way we had come.

The flitting shadows of the woods were welcome now. I was glad to be in the coolness and the quiet. I did not understand what it was about Gabe that so excited me when I was around him. For all his placidity on the surface, there were torrents of passion within him. He was a man who cared — cared deeply — about things. He cared about these hills and woods. He cared about his family and what had been done to them. And, yes, he could hate fervently, too, as he hated the Andrewses — not any specific member of the family, but the family in general, and what they represented to him.

I had come to the creek, with its stepping stones. I crossed gingerly, keeping my eyes on my feet, so that I did not notice anything on the opposite bank until I had crossed over and was on the grassy path again. I paused to look at my watch. It was almost a quarter after one. The time had gone swiftly.

I looked up then, and saw the figure of a man just before me on the path. My thoughts went instantly to that shadowy, watching figure I had seen last night, who had seemed to be following me.

For a long moment he only stared back at me. His face was expressionless, but I saw that his eyes had a gentle look, not at all threatening.

He spoke first, nodding his head and saying, 'Afternoon, miss.'

I stammered, 'Good afternoon,' in reply.

'You'll be going back to the Andrews house?' he asked. I nodded and he said, 'These woods can be dangerous if you don't know them. Take care.'

With that he went around me, careful to keep a distance between us, and began to cross the creek. I looked after him, feeling utterly foolish for that brief moment of alarm. He was only a kindly old man with gentle eyes, a threat to no one. What must I have looked like, staring wide-eyed at him? I watched his bright plaid shirt disappear into the trees. He did not look back. No doubt he realized he had frightened me.

I was soon home. I took Zeke back to

his kennel. He did not seem to mind going, and seemed eager to rejoin his companions.

Coming back around the house, I saw the magnolia tree and the devil's dance on the lawn. It never ceased to draw my attention, that ring of bare earth in the midst of all the green.

Doctor Williams was there when I came in. I went up to Mrs. Andrews's room, where he was just preparing to leave. He greeted me cordially.

'I've told the two patients they may get up this afternoon and have dinner downstairs if they like,' he said, 'but I've advised them against any hikes in the woods, particularly to look for mushrooms.'

'Williams, you old fool,' Mrs. Andrews snapped. 'You can quit harping on those mushrooms. You know as well as I that I never made any such mistake.'

He did not argue the point with her, but gave me a quick glance. Mrs. Maywood had come in. She plumped up Mrs. Andrews's pillows and said, 'Mrs. Hollis called to see if her Nellie was over here. She wandered off somewhere and Mrs. Hollis doesn't know where.'

'Probably walked into town,' Doctor Williams said. 'As I recall, Nellie has an affinity for soda fountain sweets.' He turned his attention to me. 'By the by, that nephew of mine has decided he'll stay around for a few days. I guess that will please Laura May Hollis. She's been throwing Nellie at his head since he got here.'

His eyes twinkled, telling me that it was not Mrs. Hollis's daughter, Nellie, for whom Phil was staying.

9

I saw the doctor out. When he had gone, I went into the parlor. I wanted some time to think quietly. It was odd. When I had first arrived, Pam had bemoaned the fact that there were no eligible and attractive young men in the area for me to meet, and now I had two to consider. Of course, neither of them had exactly proposed marriage yet, but it was plain that both of them were interested in me, and were courting me, in a manner of speaking, in their own quite different ways.

What a study in contrasts they were. Phil was light and Gabe dark, and it was more than their hair colors that those adjectives described. Phil was of a sunny disposition, bright and cheerful and polished, while Gabe's dark aura was one of swiftly changing moods, sometimes mysterious, sometimes hinting at things wild and savage. Phil was a man of the city, and Gabe would always be rooted in these woods and hills.

To any sensible girl, there was really no competition. Phil was a doctor, already established, with his own practice. He would be a good husband in the old-fashioned sense of that phrase, and a good father. The woman who married him would live eventually in a prosperous home in the suburbs.

What of the woman who married Gabe? Well, that was assuming he would marry at all, and on the face of it he did not appear to be the marrying kind. And if he did marry, that poor woman would be inheriting something far from placid. She would have to be nimble to get around those moods of his. There would be storm after storm, and he would not, during all of them, be at her side. He would provide for his family, no doubt of that — he was honest and hard-working — but it would not be in a prosperous suburban home. She would have a frustrating, nerve-wracking life, rarely calm; and even when it was calm, there would be the waiting for those passions simmering inside him to boil over.

It was hardly a competition, I told myself, again rising and making my way up to Pam's room. Any sensible woman would know which of the two to encourage.

★   ★   ★

Dinner was something of an occasion, with the two bed patients able to dress and come down for the meal. The sight of the two of them reminded me that the mystery of their poisoning was still unsolved. They had come close to death, and no one could say satisfactorily how or why.

I put these thoughts aside, however, and applied myself to making the meal as pleasant as possible. Mrs. Maywood had outdone herself in preparing a variety of delicious dishes, and the mood was truly festive. Even my spirits, which had been flagging all day, rose to the occasion.

'We're having champagne tonight,' Mrs. Andrews announced as Mrs. Maywood brought the bottle in. 'This is to be a bubbly night.' She poured the shimmering pale liquid into glasses and we toasted one another, and got a little giddy. By the time we had emptied our glasses, the atmosphere around our table was like the bubbles in the champagne, light and bright and gay.

That bubble, however, was doomed to burst. We were just finishing dinner and had not yet had coffee, when Mrs. Maywood came to say that Mrs. Andrews was wanted on the phone. 'It's Mrs. Hollis,' Mrs. Maywood said. 'She sounds like she's crying.'

Mrs. Andrews hurried out to the phone. She was back in little more than a minute or two, looking shaken. 'That was Laura May,' she said, pausing dramatically just inside the door. 'She's fit to be tied, crying and carrying on something fierce. Nellie never came back. She's just disappeared, and Laura May has called the sheriff. She thinks something has happened to the girl. And Laura is beside herself, and wants someone to come be with her.'

★ ★ ★

As it turned out, it was I who went to Laura May. Someone had to be with her and I did not feel it would be wise for Pam or Mrs. Andrews to go, both being still shaky from their recent ordeals. For the same reason, Mrs. Maywood had to stay with them, and Annie, unfortunately, could not be counted as much help in a crisis.

So I went to the Hollis house. I was not the only one. Mrs. Williams was already there and had pretty well taken charge. 'I've made coffee,' she said. 'There's gallons of it in the kitchen. I expect we'll all want it before we're through.' It had begun to rain outside when I arrived. It was a stark contrast to the festive atmosphere we had been enjoying at dinner.

'And Mrs. Hollis?' I asked. It was Mrs. Williams who had let me in when I arrived. There were already a number of men outside. Three of them wore the uniforms of Sheriff's deputies, and I recognized Doctor Williams and his nephew, Phil, but the men were all absorbed in conversation and I had come in without speaking to any of them.

'She's in bed. The doctor gave her a sedative, but it hasn't knocked her out yet. Mollie Rogers and Glenda Wagner are with her.'

The kitchen's bright light belied the gloom that had settled upon the house. Doctor Williams came in the back door and helped himself to a cup of coffee.

'Hasn't anyone any idea what's happened to the girl?' I asked. 'She can't have just disappeared.'

'She seems to have done precisely that,' he said. 'Her mother was here all day. She said she went out to the back terrace to read her mail when it came. The sheriff's got that pinpointed to one o'clock, or not more than five after. He's already talked to Fred Hughes, the man who delivers this mail route. And Laura says she came back in from the terrace at one-thirty, because the one-thirty news was just coming on the radio when she came into the kitchen. Nellie was in the kitchen when Laura went outside, and gone when she came back, and that's the last anyone's seen or heard of her.'

'Was Nellie in the habit of going off like that without saying anything?'

'Not according to Laura May. She says she never went anywhere without telling her mother, and I think that's probably right. She was not a bold girl.'

'There's one thing we can be fairly certain of,' I said. 'We know she likely wasn't kidnapped.'

'What makes you say that?' the doctor asked, so intensely that I knew that possibility was already being discussed by the men outside.

'Her mother couldn't have been more than a few feet or yards away. The weather was warm earlier in the day, so the windows would have been open, and probably the door as well. If there had been any sort of struggle, or Nellie had cried out, she'd certainly have been heard, and Nellie is a big enough girl she'd certainly have managed to scream

162

or make some sort of struggle if someone came in.'

'Unless it was someone she knew,' Doctor Williams said.

'Ralph!' Mrs. Williams looked shocked.

'It's been known to happen to other people. But I'd better tell the sheriff what you said, in case he hasn't thought of that himself.' He went out into the rain, now falling in earnest. Mrs. Williams and I exchanged looks, but we did not speak of what her husband had suggested. There was not much we could say. Neither of us wanted to put into words the sort of things we were thinking, and our attempts at optimism sounded oddly hollow.

'She's probably taken a notion to go somewhere, and got caught in the rain,' Mrs. Williams said, but the suggestion fell flat. It was difficult to think where and why Nellie had been trapped for nine hours, for it was now almost ten o'clock — and the rain hadn't started to fall more than an hour earlier.

A group of men came in, headed by the sheriff. Phil was among them and he came directly across the kitchen to me, taking my hand in his.

I was introduced to the sheriff. He had a gruff manner that seemed rather assumed. I wondered if he often had missing girls to track down. He held up a ring of keys. 'These belong to anybody here?' he asked.

I shook my head, as did the others around the room, glancing at one another.

'Where did they come from?' Mrs. Williams asked.

'They was in the mud alongside the front steps,' he said, his tone giving the words a significance that was not hard to grasp. If someone had taken Nellie, it might be the same someone who had dropped the keys.

The sheriff gave the keys to Mrs. Williams. 'You'd best ask Laura if she recognizes these.' The doctor's wife bustled off toward the bedroom.

'Looks like we had better put a party together,' the sheriff said. 'We'll have to go looking for her.'

'Hasn't anyone some idea of where she might have gone?' I asked.

He looked at me as if wishing I might pull the answer to that one out of a hat. 'No telling. She might have just gone out for a walk, and been hurt, and not able to get back. Or she might have run away with a boyfriend. There's all sorts of possibilities.'

He did not enumerate the other possibilities, but the fact that the men in the room did not look directly at one another told pretty clearly what they were thinking.

'Rain's washed away any tracks,' the sheriff added, answering that question before anyone need voice it. 'Hers, or any others that might be there.'

Mrs. Williams came back to inform us that Mrs. Hollis could not identify the keys. The sheriff looked at them for a long minute. He might have been willing them to speak, but they did not, and he thrust them into his pocket. It was not hard to see that they were the most important clue as to what had happened to the missing girl.

The sheriff turned to one of his deputies and said, 'Better start rounding up all the men you can. We got a lot of woods to look through. Have them meet back here by, say, eleven o'clock.'

'Perhaps we could put up some sandwiches and thermoses of coffee,' I suggested. 'I'll go back to the Andrews house and bring what things I can from there.'

'Good idea,' the sheriff said.

I gave Phil a wan smile. I felt certain this was a far cry from the way he had envisioned himself spending his vacation, but there was no reluctance in his pleasant features.

'I hope,' I said as I started toward the door, 'that she's only been hurt and is just lying out there waiting to be found.'

'Not the best of situations either,' the sheriff said.

Of course I had spoken without thinking. I was not as well acquainted with these hills and woods as the local people, but I saw at once what he meant. They could be dangerous even by day. If Nellie had somehow hurt herself, and was lying helplessly in the woods, she was at the mercy of I hardly knew what kinds of

166

animals — bears, certainly, and snakes, and wild dogs. I thought of the dogs that had attacked me. What if I had been helpless on the ground, with a broken ankle? Would I have lived to tell the tale?

There were other dangers, too. Hungry Hill, with its web of sinkholes into which even a native might carelessly step, and that obscene pond with its black-and-green slime.

And beyond those dangers was still another, far uglier to consider.

I went out, and as I hurried through the rain to my car, I remembered leaving Doctor Williams's house the night before, and that glimpse of a man along the drive, so fleeting that I had not been able to recognize him, but I was sure he had been watching me as I left.

Had he watched Nellie, too? Watched, and . . . something more?

10

It was nearly midnight by the time I got back to the Hollis house. I'd had to explain, first to Mrs. Andrews and then to Pam, what had occurred. Both suggested at once that they should go back with me, but I persuaded them that there was as yet not much they could do, and they settled for my promises to keep them informed if any news developed.

I took three thermos jugs of coffee provided by Mrs. Maywood, as well as a large basket of sandwiches she and Annie had put together hurriedly. Mrs. Andrews brought a large jug of whisky, too, and gave it to me.

'It's an ugly night,' she said. 'Those men will need this to keep them warm. And if Preacher Stevens's wife is there, you tell her this is medicinal.'

I took blankets too, and an armload of extra coats in case some of the men came back and wanted to change into dry clothes.

As I drove along the winding country road on my return trip, I saw a light flash in some woods near the road. I braked the car and came to a stop. The light flashed again, and then a second and a third flickered beyond that first one.

I realized then this was the search party scouring the woods. The rain beat down heavily on the car's windshield, and I felt pity for those men, already chilled and wet. I started up the car again and went on.

Nellie, of course, must be wet and chilled, too. I would have liked to believe that all of this was some harmless misunderstanding. One read of such things. A group of boys, presumed lost, were found sleeping in a lean-to in their backyard. Or a girl was thought kidnapped, only to turn up in some distant city to which she had run away. I could not quite imagine Nellie running away, though. She was too much the delicate flower. Running away suggested a weed, or even a thistledown floating gaily on the breeze. Nellie was a violet, or a lily of the valley, and they did not travel far on impulse. Yet she had gone of her own accord; she almost surely must have, to have disappeared so silently.

'Unless it was someone she knew,' Doctor Williams had said.

There it was, the ugliest thought of all the ugly thoughts. If Nellie had not just run away, or if she had not just gone for a stroll and hurt herself — and how far could she have strolled in that half-hour before her mother discovered her missing? — if some mischief had been done by someone, then it must have been someone she knew. Someone most of these people knew. Perhaps even someone I knew. And they did say, did they not, that most molestations, most murders and crimes of violence, were perpetrated not by strangers, but by acquaintances?

I saw him again just then — that lurking, shadowy figure. I slowed to make the turn into the Hollises, and there once again was the dark shadow of a man hiding behind a tree.

I braked hard, making the car slide to a

stop. This time, I thought, he was not going to disappear like a puff of smoke from a cigarette. I leapt from the car, too concerned with the thought that he might be connected with Nellie's disappearance even to contemplate what sort of danger I might be putting myself into.

He was not where I had seen him. The trees came right up to the road here. He had only to take a few steps and be lost among them. I walked on for a few feet, past the tree where I thought I had seen him — and from behind it, a hand shot out to seize my wrist.

'Gabe!' My voice was a cracked whisper that barely made it past my lips.

'Be quiet,' he ordered in a whisper as well. He pulled me into the shadow of the tree. I threw my head back, looking wildly up into his eyes. I was too terrified to dream of trying to free myself from his grip.

'What's happened up there?' he asked, nodding his head in the direction of the Hollis house.

Somehow I managed to find enough voice to say, 'Nellie is missing.'

'How?'

I told him what little I knew. Once he interrupted to murmur, 'It was true, then,' but that was all he said.

'The men are forming search parties,' I concluded. 'Shouldn't you be with them?'

He laughed — a cynical, bitter sound that seemed to reverberate from the wet leaves overhead. 'Do you think they'd let me help? Have you forgotten what I am?'

'You're a man.'

'Not in their eyes. To them, I'm a Melungeon. Don't be sorry for me. It doesn't bother me. I got used to it a long time ago.'

He was lying, of course. It did bother him, and because of that I felt a great surge of emotion going out from me to him. I wanted to comfort him, to make up for the stupid prejudice that had caused him this bitterness.

'What are you doing here in the woods, anyway?' he asked. 'Haven't you learned your lesson?'

'I saw you in my headlights, hiding behind a tree. I didn't know who it was. I came to investigate.'

'All by yourself? You're a very brave girl.'

'No, only impulsive.'

He was silent for a long time, staring into the distance. I could see that he was thinking hard. I waited, looking up at his face. It appeared stern in the near darkness, lighted faintly from behind by the lights from up at the house. There was something sad and tortured in his expression. I could not define the emotion he aroused in me, but I knew that I had a burning desire to help him in some way, and that I did not mind standing with him like this in the dark and the rain.

He suddenly looked down at me and caught me staring. Our eyes met. He said, quite softly, 'I think you really care — about me, about all this stupidity.' I did not try to answer. After a moment, he whispered, 'Thank you.'

Then, suddenly, I was in his arms, crushed against him, and his lips were on mine, hungry, demanding. I forgot the night, the rain; forgot the unhappiness waiting at that house nearby. I was oblivious to everything but this man whose hard body warmed mine and whose lips made a slave of me. I clung to him weakly, not able to trust my legs to bear my weight, and at the same time feeling weightless, as if I were soaring upward, higher and higher, into the clouds above.

He released me finally and gave a low, little laugh of barely contained excitement. His eyes flashed and his breath was ragged. This was not a cool man of placid affection, but a man whose passions simmered close to the boiling point. I half expected him to fling me to the ground and fall upon me. I don't think I would have fought him.

But he held me away from him. 'I'd better get out of here, before somebody else sees me. They'll think I had something to do with her disappearing. Do you think . . . ?' He stopped himself before he had finished that question. 'No, I'll not put you to that test. Go up to the house. And stop taking chances. You could be hurt, running through the woods like this at night.'

'What are you going to do?'

'Find Nellie.' He led me back to where my car still sat, motor running, door open. Had it been seen by any of those searchers, they would surely have counted me another victim.

Victim? Not a nice word to use, I told myself as I got into the car. Gabe was gone, disappearing again into the trees, leaving me trembling and shaken, and not by fear alone.

11

They found no trace of Nellie during that black, eerie night. The men came back in little bunches to down numerous cups of hot coffee with the occasional whiskey and to dry out a little, and then they went out again. But by dawn, even the hardiest had been forced to go home for a spell, to snatch a little sleep and some hot food.

They regrouped again at nine, more of them than there had been the night before. The rain had slowed to little more than a descending mist, but you could hardly see twenty feet in front of you for the fog that came with it. That made the search more difficult but not much slower, because this morning they planned to comb the ground, searching in a nearly solid line, inch by inch, for any clue.

This time I went with the searchers, as did several other women. It was no heroism on my part. I felt I needed to be stirring. I had slept in snatches and starts on an easy chair in the front parlor of Mrs. Hollis's house, and the idea of walking in the rain for a spell actually seemed welcome.

Nor was there any particular need for me at the house. Throughout the night, local women had been arriving in a steady stream, some merely checking in to see if everything was all right, and others staying to take over the responsibility of coffee-making, food-preparing and, in general, waiting.

Laura May herself had emerged from the bedroom an hour or so earlier. She looked pale and wasted, but I was surprised to learn that beneath that simpering, sugary exterior she had rather admirable self-control. She made a valiant effort at graciousness toward her numerous 'guests' so that one might have thought she was only having some of the neighbors in for brunch.

By now the search had become grimmer. The possibilities as to what might have happened to the missing girl had sadly narrowed themselves in everyone's minds. No one talked of her maybe having run away somewhere, although of course there was still the outside chance that she might have done so.

During the night, relatives and friends had been carefully questioned. None could offer any help. There had been a glimmer of hope when it had been uncovered that Nellie had a 'boyfriend' whom she had seen from time to time, apparently without her mother's knowledge, but young Jamie Hudson had been at work that afternoon in a local garage, in plain view of so many co-workers and customers that there was not the slightest possibility of his having been with Nellie.

So the search went on. We were all bundled up against the day's chill and the wind that lurched over the hills. I walked with my head down, not only against the chill, but so that I could watch the ground carefully. I could not help thinking of the thousands of acres of woodland and hills like this that surrounded us. Would we have to search them all?

I came to the crest of a hill and the wind met me with gusto, yanking at my coat as if urging me to come along with it on its swift travel down the embankment.

I was grateful to notice, as the morning wore on, that the weather had begun to clear. The rain stopped altogether and there was a glimmer of light through the mist. Then the mist was lifting, until finally we could see clearly. Our spirits lifted a little with the fog. We were still searching as before, watching the ground at our feet, but at least we felt less oppressed.

The further we got into the hills, however, the more difficult the going became, and I could begin to appreciate more fully the fact that much of this country was still wild. I clawed my way over huge boulders, my feet slipping out from under me on the wet grass, my breath coming more and more unevenly.

At last I had to stop. I had been going on nervous energy, but even that was giving out. I was simply not accustomed to scrambling about on these hills. I dropped back and saw that the two men on either side of me, perhaps each fifteen feet from me, immediately moved a little closer together to close the gap. They were both local men who walked in a curiously slouching way, but whose sharp eyes seemed to miss nothing.

I found a huge boulder at the foot of a little overhanging bluff and sat down on it, heedless of what I might be doing to my coat. My feet felt numb in my shoes.

Someone whistled. I looked around and saw nothing, but a moment later there was a scrambling on the bluff above me, and as I stood, Gabe appeared over its edge and dropped beside me. 'I thought I saw you fall back,' he said. He scrutinized me. 'You look exhausted.'

'I am tired, a little. I just began to realize it myself.'

'And no sign of Nellie?'

'None.' His question told me that he had found nothing as well.

'There you are,' someone said, and we looked to see Phil coming toward us. 'I was just asking my uncle for you. We thought you ought to take a rest.' He came up and stood just beside me. The two men eyed each other in a suspicious fashion. I introduced them.

'Goins,' Phil said. 'I've heard of you.'

Gabe sent a mocking look from him to me. 'The devil you say,' he murmured.

'What are you doing here, anyway?' Phil asked. I think he meant to be protective of me, but he only sounded rude.

Gabe smiled as if he had not noticed the rudeness. Of course I saw that he had, and minded very much, and again that protective instinct of mine leapt up to him.

'Keeping an eye on Miss Collins. She has an unfortunate habit of wandering off into the woods, and I like to see that nothing amiss happens to her. But I see she has a protector now, so maybe I won't be needed.'

He turned and gave me a mock bow, his eyes dark and sardonic-looking as they met mine. 'Take care,' he said, and without waiting for a reply he was gone, scrambling up the hillside and out of sight.

I was angry with Phil for his rudeness,

and would have said a few sharp words, but when I turned, I saw Doctor Williams approaching. He looked quite out of breath, and I wondered if he had been to bed at all.

'So you found her. We've been looking for you, young lady. I want you to take yourself home to bed and get some rest, and that's a doctor's order.'

I was not inclined to argue the point. As tired as I was just now, I doubted that I was any longer functioning with efficiency, and a careless searcher might be far worse than one less searcher.

I stood, brushing off my coat. 'Is there any news at all?'

'The sheriff's found the man those keys belong to. Local man by the name of Mullins.'

'A Melungeon name.' The doctor nodded.

That piece of news saddened me. I could not help thinking of Gabe, and how it might add to his bitterness and unhappiness if this were found to be the act of a Melungeon. It would certainly add to the local prejudice and resentment against the Melungeons. People never liked to blame individuals for anything really awful; that made it much too human, and too close to home. They preferred to blame categories, races, tribes. If a Melungeon were somehow responsible for Nellie's disappearance, it would be all Melungeons, and not one individual man with a warped mind, who were blamed.

'Has he said anything?'

'They're his keys, all right; he admits that. He says he lost them, and he was up at the house the day before replacing a broken windowpane for Mrs. Hollis, and she bears that out. So he might have lost the keys then. There's no way of saying for sure yet. The sheriff has him down at the house now, talking to him.'

'Then, perhaps . . . ' I paused. I had been about to say 'Perhaps this will soon all be over,' but I didn't want to hope for *that* ending to the story, not even by implication. I let the sentence remain unfinished.

'I'll walk you back,' Phil said.

'No, you're needed here far more.' I

tried not to mind that he had to be told that. Something of my thoughts must have showed in my voice, however, because he did not argue the point.

I walked back quickly the way I had come so slowly. By now the sun was out, and the air was warming. The men would soon be shedding their coats. It would make walking a little easier.

I did not mean to intrude upon the sheriff, nor try to steal a glimpse of the man he was questioning. I haven't that macabre sort of curiosity that some people seem to have, the kind of curiosity that sends them scrambling to watch at the first report of a forest fire or an automobile accident.

I could not help seeing the men, though. They were outside as I came down the hill. There was a small cluster of them, including the sheriff and one of his deputies, and with them was a little man in plaid shirt. He was by one of the windows of the house, evidently pantomiming how he had put the glass in and how he might have lost the keys that had been found.

I recognized the shirt at once, although there may have been scores of identical shirts in the area for all I knew, but I quickened my steps and as I came closer I saw without any doubt that the man the sheriff was questioning was the same little man I had met in the woods yesterday afternoon — not these woods we were searching here, but all the way on the other side of the Andrews place, between there and Gabe's home. This was the same man who had warned me to be careful of the path.

I went directly to the group of men. The sheriff looked up as I approached, and several pairs of eyes turned in my direction. I could see that the sheriff did not exactly welcome an intrusion just now, but he gave me a quick 'Morning, miss.'

'Good morning,' I greeted him in reply. 'I'm sorry to intrude, but is this gentleman the one who lost his keys?'

The sheriff's eyes darkened. Probably he was wondering how I had heard of this so quickly, but he nodded. 'Yes, this is Mister Mullins.'

'Then I can save you some time. I don't know when Mister Mullins lost his keys, but I do know when he did not lose them. I saw him yesterday afternoon, just about one fifteen.'

There was a stirring of interest among the men. I glanced at Mister Mullins. His kindly face was impassive. It was impossible to tell what he was thinking.

'Where was this?' the sheriff asked.

I told him. I could follow the mental calculations he was making. I had made them myself as soon as I had spotted Mister Mullins's plaid shirt and realized who he was.

'He wouldn't have had time,' the deputy said. 'Even if a man was running all the way, that's twenty, twenty-five minutes from here, and old Mullins here couldn't run that distance. If he had, the girl would've had to carry him off, not the other way round.'

The sheriff looked disappointed, and I supposed that he was. He had an ugly problem on his hands, and it would have made things a great deal better for him if he had solved it so quickly.

'If he'd a come in a car,' the Sheriff said, not eager to give up.

The deputy, who gave every indication of being pleased to see Mister Mullins exonerated, said, 'Everybody knows Mullins ain't got a car. You know that yourself.'

The Sheriff scowled at me. 'You sure of that time? It could have been ten minutes either way, couldn't it?'

I shook my head firmly. 'No, I had just looked at my watch. It was one-thirteen, to be exact. And my watch is accurate. You can see for yourself. I haven't set it since then.' I held my hand up so that they could read the time on my watch. Several of them compared times. We were all within a minute of one another.

The sheriff seemed ready to concede the point. 'Well,' he said to Mullins, 'I guess that clears that up. You better be careful with your keys in the future, old man.'

I breathed a sigh of relief and accepted the sheriff's less-than-enthusiastic thanks, and went inside to collect my things. When I came out again a few minutes later, the men had disappeared, presumably taking up the search for clues to Nellie's disappearance.

That was, all of them had gone except for Mister Mullins. He was waiting at the bottom of the steps, his hat in his hand. He was waiting for me. As I came down the steps, he walked toward me. 'I want to thank ye, miss,' he said, 'for clearing me with the sheriff.'

'I didn't do anything but tell him the truth,' I said, 'and that's not something one should expect to be thanked for.' I paused and then said, 'You mustn't mind that they questioned you. Everyone is worried and upset, and they just want to learn what has happened.'

He nodded his head. 'And so would I like to know. So would I.'

I had the impression that, for all his gentle-seeming manner, Mister Mullins would not deal kindly with the person who had been responsible for all this, should he learn who that was. It was a feeling I'd had among the many men searching the woods.

I think by now, everyone felt inwardly

that someone had done something to the girl, and that sort of thing went violently against the grain of these people. This was not the big city, where people might walk by a crime being done and ignore it. These people cared, and cared deeply.

I thought that if some one man were responsible, had done something to the missing girl, that it would be far better for him if it were the sheriff and his deputies who learned his identity, and not those men out combing the hills.

12

It was something of a relief to be back at Home Acres, although that relief was clouded by the knowledge that Nellie was still missing. She had been gone more than twenty-four hours now, not so terribly long for a healthy young girl — and Nellie was hardly much more than a girl — but it was long enough to leave everyone certain that she had not just forgotten to come back, or something equally harmless. No, she was certainly hurt, and that was taking the most optimistic view.

I was exhausted, though, and glad to have a rest. Even Mrs. Maywood took a gentle attitude toward me, hurriedly putting together a hot lunch for me and serving it herself. Pam and Mrs. Andrews had had a more difficult task, perhaps, than mine. They'd had simply to sit and wait for news, while I had at least been in the search, doing something, however futile.

Both of them sat with me while I did more than justice to Mrs. Maywood's hot ham sandwich and a broth thick with garden vegetables, and they asked their questions, restraining themselves as much as possible to give me time to eat.

Between bites of food, I answered them as best I could, although in fact I had little enough to tell them. The search, painstakingly combing every inch of woods and fields, took hours, but the telling of it only minutes.

'And still not a single clue?' Pam asked.

'It's the work of spirits,' Mrs. Andrews muttered darkly. 'Melungeons. They'll never find that girl.'

I had a flash of resentment that she should, without any evidence, lay this business at the feet of the Melungeons. I knew that at least two Melungeons, Mister Mullins and Gabe, were as concerned as anybody else over Nellie's disappearance.

I was too tired now, however, to argue with Mrs. Andrews. I pretended not to hear what she said.

191

'Nothing at all,' I said to Pam. 'It's as if the ground had simply swallowed her up and . . . ' I stopped in mid-sentence.

'Lord,' I said, a light breaking in my mind, 'Could that be . . . ?' I jumped up from the table, pushing the food aside. I had forgotten all about being hungry or tired. 'I've got to go out.'

'Chris, what on earth?' Pam jumped up too, looking justifiably startled.

'I've just thought of something. It's crazy, but I can't help thinking . . . I have an idea where Nellie is.'

'But you can't go out on your own,' Mrs. Andrews said, the two of them hurrying after me into the hall. 'Call one of the men and tell them whatever it is you've thought of.'

'Call whom? Every available man is already searching the woods on the other side of here, toward the Hollises, but no one has searched our hills and woods, on this side.'

'But it's miles from the Hollises to here,' Mrs. Andrew said. 'Nellie wouldn't have walked that far just to be going for a walk; and if she had, and had gotten this far, she'd have stopped by here for a visit. She wouldn't have gone right on past.'

'If she was just out strolling. But she may not have been. She may have been with someone. There may have been some reason for hurrying by here without stopping.'

'Where do you think she is, then?' Pam asked.

'Where would a girl just disappear so that no one would see her; so that it would seem like the earth had just swallowed her up?'

'Hungry Hill,' Mrs. Andrews said in a whisper.

I nodded. 'Don't worry; I'll take Zeke, and I'll keep a stick in front of me. I may be chasing a will-o-the-wisp, but I have a feeling . . . '

I was grateful the weather had broken. My fatigue had vanished in the teeth of this new excitement, but I might have felt differently if it were still cold and raining.

Zeke was as enthusiastic as ever at the idea of a walk, but there was something earnest about the way he stayed close by me, sniffing regularly at the ground as if he, too, knew the purpose of our hike, and had put his mind to helping solve the mystery.

Near the kennels was an old-fashioned clothesline with props to hold it up. I took one of the props, a sturdy pole almost as tall as I was. I wanted to take no unnecessary risks, and this one could not only be used to feel out any sinkholes or snakes that might lie before me, but could be used as a weapon as well. If, I amended quickly, I should need a weapon.

I found my way to Hungry Hill with little difficulty, taking a wrong path just once. As we neared that part of the woods, Zeke grew increasingly less enthusiastic. He seemed to realize where we were going, and he plainly did not like the idea. His instincts warned him of danger, and I found myself thinking perhaps I was a fool not to share his reluctance. He came with me, though, his forays into the thickets becoming fewer and fewer, until he was staying fast by my side.

We came to the fence where I had tried

to elude the wild dog pack. I climbed over and Zeke found his way through, rejoining me on the other side. I started up the hill and stopped when someone shouted.

I turned and saw Gabe hurrying toward us. He looked angry, and as he came up to me, he said, 'What in the devil are you doing out here?'

'Looking for Nellie. It suddenly occurred to me that if she had gotten lost here, there'd be no trace of her.'

'That's foolishness. Nellie wouldn't have come here. She knew better.'

I noticed he had used the past tense. It cast a gloom over me. 'That's because everyone has started out with the assumption, or maybe the hope, that Nellie just went out for a walk of her own volition, and so they've started searching around her house and working out from there. But the destination might not have been Nellie's choice.'

He took a moment to consider what I had said. 'I don't like you climbing around here. It's too dangerous.'

'But she might be here.'

'Then you go back and I'll look.'

He made an order of it, and although it is never pleasant to be told what to do, there was something so personal and intimate in his tone that it startled me. I was suddenly aware of him again as a man; aware of that strong magnetism he had for me.

'You've lost a button,' I said, seizing upon the first trivial, impersonal thing I saw. I put my finger on the spot where the brass button had fallen from his jacket. I wanted to replace the button for him — wanted to take care of all his needs, big and little. I looked up and was frightened a little by the intensity of his gaze. 'I want to help look, really. I'll be careful. If you like, we can stay together. I'll be safe with you.'

He relented, albeit reluctantly, and the three of us — Gabe, Zeke and myself — began to search the hillside. 'But it's a waste of time,' Gabe insisted.

He was wrong. We had been looking less than ten minutes before we found the proof of my intuition, a piece of cloth caught on a branch of a thicket.

'It's a flower print,' I said, holding the scrap of cloth up, a field of lavender violets on a white background. 'Nellie's mother said she was wearing a flower-print dress.'

'It doesn't prove anything. Anyone could have been wearing this. We don't know if it's off Nellie's dress, and we don't know how long this has been here.'

'It doesn't look like it's been here too long. And it's a woman's cloth; look at it. None of the men around here would be wearing anything like this in the woods.'

Gabe refused to agree with me that it was a scrap from Nellie's dress, but he did start to search more determinedly, so that I thought that he, too, was beginning to share my belief that Nellie was somewhere close by.

It was slow searching, because Gabe would not let me go on my own, but made me follow close at his heels. He kept his eyes on the ground, alert for danger from sinkholes, and he used the pole I had brought with me for the same purpose, poking the ground before us with it. Even Zeke stayed close at hand, sniffing the ground and watching the two of us carefully. His tail no longer wagged, and he clearly did not like being here.

The time dragged. I was almost ready to suggest to Gabe that we give it up for a bad attempt when we came upon a freshly collapsed sinkhole, a yawning mouth of earth big enough for a car to have fallen through.

'Careful,' Gabe said, holding me behind him. 'The rest of the ground around it may be like eggshells.'

We approached that cavern slowly, Gabe thumping the ground soundly before each step. The ground held, and we came closer and closer to the edge.

Gabe stopped suddenly in front of me, and stiffened. I could actually see his shoulders go rigid. I knew that he had seen down into that hole.

'Gabe?' I said, touching his arm.

'Don't look.'

But I had to look. I stepped up beside him and leaned forward to look down into that yawning cavern.

She was down there, arms and legs at impossible angles, amidst a heap of rubble, earth and rocks that had fallen in with her. Even from where we were, I recognized the print of her dress, the same as the scrap I still held in my hand.

Gabe said, 'I'll have to go down there.'

I grabbed his arm tightly. 'Oh Gabe, no.'

'She might be alive.'

He was right, of course. She might be alive, and if she were, then she was clinging to life with a slender thread, and every second counted for life and death. 'How will you get back out?'

'I won't, until you get the sheriff up here with ropes. You go back to the Andrews place, it's closest, and get hold of the sheriff or whatever men you can get hold of first and fastest.'

He had taken off his jacket as he spoke. He saw the frightened look on my face and said, 'Don't worry. We Melungeons are part spirit.'

Then, nimble as a cat, he was at the edge and stooping, swinging himself over. In an instant he was within, dropping to the ground below. He landed in a crouch, falling, but righted himself quickly. He looked up to reassure me.

'Is she . . . ?' I couldn't bring myself to say the word.

'Go for the sheriff. And be careful.'

I did as he had said, but when I had gone a few feet, I came back. I wanted to say . . . I don't know now what. I wanted to see him again, buried as he was in the very bowels of the earth. I wanted to tell him I loved him, that I would not be long. I wanted . . .

But whatever I wanted, it died on my lips. I came to the edge, not so near that I would have blocked the light — I was not brave enough to go that close. I leaned forward to look in, and I saw him bending over her, not over her twisted body, but over one outstretched hand. He was prying the fingers apart, and in a second he removed something from them. It flashed in the light as he examined it; then it was gone, dropped into his pocket, and he was turning to look at her face.

I stepped back quickly, where he could not see me. Something was churning inside me. I did not faint, although I thought for a moment that I might.

Rather, there was the feeling of the earth slipping away from me, as if I, too, were falling through it into the depths below.

The moment passed. A gust of wind sent a strand of my hair across my face. I pushed it back, and at the same time I pushed back my thoughts, thoughts of the button missing from Gabe's jacket, the jacket I held in my hands — thoughts of the button he had found in that girl's hand and had removed and hidden.

I turned and ran, ran as if all the devils of that hill were in hot pursuit; and Zeke, no less eager than I to be off that hill, ran wildly before me. We startled a flock of birds — quail, I think — and sent them rushing upward into the sky, crying in anger and alarm.

13

Looking back, it seems incredible that after the nearly sleepless night I had spent, exhausted as I had been, that I was able to run that distance. But fear drove me — fear greater than any dangers that might have been in my path.

As to the latter, fortune chose to spare me those, and I reached the house, out of breath and nearly dropping, without suffering any misadventures along the way. I did not think of putting Zeke in the kennel, and he was so caught up in my emotions that he ran straight to the house with me.

They must have been waiting and watching for my return, because even as the dog and I bounded up the steps, Pam threw the front door open.

'Chris, what is it?' she cried. 'You look scared out of your wits.'

My breath was a fire burning in my chest. I was barely able to get out the words. 'The sheriff — Hungry Hill — we found Nellie.'

I fell into Pam's arms. I had used all the reserves of strength that I possessed, and what happened during the next hour or so was a blur to me. I was helped to a sofa in the parlor — I refused to be put to bed, where I would be out of contact with things — and the sheriff was sent for. He must have been near the phone at the Hollises, because it seemed only a few minutes before he was there in the parlor, questioning me.

I told him, still gasping for breath, where to find Gabe, and that he was with Nellie. I did not mention what I had seen. I had kept his jacket in my arms, even when Pam had helped me to the sofa, and it was over me now as if to keep me warm, although I was not at all chilled. I wanted no one else to have occasion to examine it until — but I did not know what it was I meant to do. I only knew that I could not easily point the finger of blame at Gabe. There must be some explanation, I kept telling myself. There must!

I would have gone with the sheriff and his men, but Pam and Mrs. Andrews would not hear of it. 'They'll find him' Pam said. 'And besides, you'd be more of a hindrance than a help. Look at you; you're as weak as a kitten still.'

She was right, needless to say, and I allowed myself to be dissuaded. I lay on the sofa, clutching that rough woolen jacket of Gabe's about me, and tried to make some sense out of my scrambled thoughts. Zeke, who had come in with me and been immediately forgotten by everyone, stared up at me anxiously, ill at ease in the house.

Why had Gabe been on Hungry Hill this afternoon, I kept wondering, when everyone else was searching for Nellie elsewhere? Mere chance? Or had he some reason to think or know that she was there? Might he have been watching, in case someone did come to look for her there? And I couldn't forget that he had tried to discourage me from searching the hill.

I had talked to Gabe last night, and he had seemed as worried as everyone else about the missing girl. It could have been mere chance that he was at Hungry Hill this afternoon, and it was he who had found her — although, of course, he could hardly have pretended not to, with me there. The chance would have been too great that I might see her, and know he had lied.

I told myself that I was being unfair to entertain these suspicions, but suspicions, once they have been spawned, are not easily dispelled.

And, there was that button . . .

★   ★   ★

It seemed to be an eternity later when the men came back from the hill. How they got those two out of the ground, I have no idea, nor do I know what explanations Gabe offered for how we found the girl. All I know is that much later there was a commotion and the sound of a great many people — a great many men — moving about.

Something was carried past the parlor door, something lying on a makeshift stretcher and covered with a raincoat. I thought, in a moment of panic, *Gabe!* But almost at once I knew it was Nellie, and not Gabe, under that coat. I saw the Sheriff go by with Doctor Williams, hurrying with a dark look on his face. I had forgotten for the moment that they would want to talk to me, and it was just as well. My shattered nerves were not up to being questioned.

Mrs. Andrews came to look in on me and bring me up to date. I think it was less a concern for me than a desire to escape the area where the grim activity was going on in the rear of the house.

Doctor Williams came at last to check on me. I believe I had known, perhaps since that first glimpse into that cavern in the ground, that Nellie was dead, so it was no surprise to have him tell me so.

'Has been for a day,' he added.

'She must have died in the fall,' Mrs. Andrews said, shaking her head sadly.

'She didn't die from any fall,' the Doctor said, feeling for my pulse as he talked. 'She was dead when she went into that hole.'

'Can you be certain of that?' I asked. I wanted to believe she had broken her neck in the fall, or died from the exposure. I wanted to believe anything but that she had been murdered, and the murderer might be someone I loved.

'Certain?' He met my eyes, and his were hard and cold. 'That poor child's throat had been cut.'

Mrs. Andrews gasped, and I felt the blood draining from my face. I bit my lips to keep from crying.

'Throat cut, and an X slashed across her forehead,' the doctor said, dropping his eyes to his watch as he counted my pulse. 'Old sign of the devil. This was a blood killing, no mistake of that.'

'The Melungeons,' Mrs. Andrews said in a hoarse voice.

14

There was a hollowness to the rest of that day. The sheriff and the doctor and all those men left — and left behind a dull void.

Doctor Williams had given me a sedative, and explicit instructions that I was to spend the rest of the day in bed. Pam, only recently quitted of her own bed, was self-elected my nurse, and with me protesting that I felt fine, she shooed me up to my room and into bed, where, still mumbling protests, I promptly fell asleep.

In truth, despite all the strain I had been under, I was yet not nearly so shaken as Mrs. Andrews was. The news of Nellie's death, followed closely by the revelation that her murder had been some sort of ritualistic affair, left that poor woman on the verge of hysteria.

I woke at seven. The sedative had worn off, although I still felt drowsy and tired.

Pam was reading. It was evening, and the light from her reading lamp created hovering shadows about my bed, shadows that would not let me be at ease.

Pam closed her book and came to the bed to ask how I felt.

'Not bad,' I said, smiling wanly, 'but I wouldn't want to tackle any dragons just now.'

'Mrs. Maywood was keeping some soup warm. I'll bring some up.' She went out, leaving me with the shadows.

I was not alone long, though. A few minutes later, the door opened and Mrs. Andrews came into the room. My first smile of greeting froze on my lips as she came closer to the bed, into the light. One look was enough to tell me how distraught she was. Her eyes were wild, and her hands clenched and unclenched themselves spasmodically, as if beyond her conscious control.

'Mrs. Andrews,' I said, sitting upright in the bed, 'are you all right?'

'All right?' She gave a desperate little laugh. 'Could I be all right, after all you've done to me?'

'I? But I don't . . . '

'They are haunting me, torturing me, and you've helped them, bringing that young man here.'

'Gabe? But he's done you no harm.'

'You little fool. You think he likes you, don't you? You don't realize he's only being nice to you to get at me, to get close to this house. He'll worm his way into your confidence and then he'll ask you to help.'

'Help with what?'

She came closer, leaning down until her face was only inches from mine. 'They are haunting me. Things have happened here, in this very house, and it's them doing it, and he's one of them. And now it's that poor girl, her throat cut — and that was their doing, too, and next it will be mine. That's why he's friendly with you; he wants you to help him kill me. And on top of everything else, you let that dog in the house, and he's ruined my carpet, my very best carpet.'

She began to cry, softly at first and then with great, heaving sobs that made her shoulders shake. It was no use being angry with her, for she was unable to reason clearly. Just at the moment, she was literally frightened out of her wits, until she'd had to lash out at someone, and I was the most obvious target. I could not help but feel sorry for her.

I scrambled out of bed, putting an arm around her, and tried to comfort her. She was crying too hard now to speak. The storm had broken within her, and she gave herself up to a torrent of sobs and tears.

'There, there. You've nothing to fear.' But my words sounded false even to my own ears. Surely we all had something to fear now.

Pam, coming back to this scene, looked astonished, but I signaled to her over Mrs. Andrews's shoulders, and she asked no questions. Between the two of us, we managed to get the older woman to her own room. She offered no resistance. She was like a child, frightened and helpless. When she was in bed, still crying, but not as hard as before, we rang for Mrs. Maywood and, leaving Pam with her, I returned to my own room.

Mrs. Andrews's accusations still rang in my ears, however. Although she had spoken hysterically, I could not entirely dismiss them. Had Gabe been friendly with me in an attempt to get closer to her and the house? It was not beyond the realm of possibility. He had admitted to me that he hated the Andrews family. He had talked of sitting for hours staring at the house, obviously coveting it. I myself had found him in the magnolia tree, watching the house. And it was common knowledge, it seemed, that there was bad blood between his family and this one.

Was he the sort to act out an age-old feud? It seemed unreasonable in a man of his intelligence and education, and yet his own words accused him. He had said he could dismiss those old hates when he was away, but that he felt differently when he came back.

I remembered that awful moment when I looked into that hole in the earth, and saw him pocket the brass button he had removed from Nellie's lifeless fingers. I went to the closet where I had hung his jacket and looked at it again. The bare spot where the button was missing seemed to leap out at me. Was it the same? I could not say for certain, but if it was different, why should he feel the need to conceal what surely must be evidence from the sheriff? And what could it be evidence of, then, if not his guilt in Nellie's death?

My thoughts were like a swarm of devils flying at me, pricking me with their poisoned lances, and flying away again, only to come back to sting me once more. I slept, and in my sleep I was haunted by visions of Gabe, and of Nellie, and of that poor frightened woman down the hall.

I woke with a chill. The night had turned cool and my window had been left open. I stole to the window to close it. The moon was up and there was no mist tonight. I could see the distant woods, a ragged line of blackness. How peaceful it all looked tonight. Yet only a day before, a girl's throat had been cut in a deliberate act of murder, and her lifeless body had been thrown into a hole in the ground, where for a day and a night the rain had fallen upon it mercilessly.

I shivered and closed the window and would have turned back to my bed, but a movement below caught my eye just then, and I stood motionless, watching. All was still, and I began to think I had imagined that flicker of movement out of the corner of my eye. Again I nearly went back to bed, and again there was movement. This time I saw the figure of a man step from the shadow of a tree, moving quickly across the moonlight that reflected on the lawn. A tall, slim figure! I did not need to see his face to know that it must be Gabe gliding silently toward the house.

He disappeared into the shadows below. My breath caught in my throat. Why? What errand could bring him here like this, stealthily, in the middle of the night? It was nearly one in the morning. I went back to the window, but nothing stirred below. I could almost believe I had dreamed that tall figure moving across the grass — but it had not been a dream, I knew that; and I must know, too, what brought him here. I was not afraid of him — not, at least, afraid of bodily harm. Whatever harm he might do me was a different sort altogether — and was already done.

I found my robe in the closet without turning on a light, and stole from my room. The house lay still and dark. It seemed to be waiting for something to happen.

I reached the stairs. Below was darkness, as black as the soul of Satan himself. I stared down, down into that blackness.

All hell suddenly broke loose. Shots rang out, crashing through the darkness, shattering stillness and glass alike. I screamed, my scream rending the air in the wake of the gunshots.

And close on the heels of my scream, a high, shrieking wail of terror from somewhere else.

15

What a blur of contrasting images is my memory of that night!

Mrs. Andrews, whose screams followed on the heels of mine, screamed again and again, hysterically. Pam, white-faced and bewildered, rushed along the hall to find me trembling at the head of the stairs.

Pam: bless her for her practical mind, and for being there to take charge, although she must have been nearly as frightened as I was.

'Chris, what on earth is it?' she cried.

'Oh, Pam, those shots . . . I . . . '

'No, that's all right, don't try to speak now.' She jerked me around and shoved me before her down the hall, and in a moment I was in my room, and she had commanded me to stay there, and left me. I heard voices, hers and Mrs. Maywood's, in the hall, murmuring briefly, and then silence.

I ran to the window, staring out at the

night. The scene was peaceful again, and still. No, not still. The dogs were muttering among themselves, and as I stood at the window, one of them began to howl, and then another, their baying drifting up to the balcony railing and the wisteria. That unreal sound struck a responsive chord in my very soul, until I wanted to howl with those frightened beasts; wail my anguish to the night winds.

'Good God, get away from those windows!'

I had not even heard Pam come in until she spoke sharply and, grabbing my arm, fairly yanked me from the windows.

'Someone's shooting up the place and you're standing there in the windows like you . . . Lord, don't cry, no don't. It's all right, I'm sorry I was so sharp. The sheriff's on his way, and he'll be here in a minute, and we're to stay inside until he arrives. No, don't cry.'

We stayed in my room, huddled together in the dark. 'Mrs. Andrews?' I asked in a whisper.

'Mrs. Maywood and Annie are both

with her. She's hysterical. The shots and your screaming — she went right off the deep end, but she was all right when I left, crying, but not screaming at least.'

When the knocker on the front door sounded and Pam got up to answer it, I didn't want her to go.

'It's the sheriff,' she said, looking out the window. 'Someone has to let him in. Come on, you go with me.'

I did, and it was the sheriff with three of his deputies. I was trundled back to bed then, and Pam was in and out to keep me abreast of things.

'No one's hanging around,' was the first announcement, delivered, I suppose, to put my mind at ease. She was over her own fright, apparently, and now that the sheriff and his men were at hand, she had no reservations in running back and forth from my room to where they were.

'Someone fired a shotgun at the attic windows in the north wing,' she informed me on her next trip. 'No harm done except for the broken glass, and a lamp that just happened to be in range.'

'The attic? But why on earth the attic?'

'Either someone was a very bad shot, or they only meant to give us a scare.'

'But why?'

'I'd say someone is trying to scare the devil out of Mrs. Andrews. And I'd say they're succeeding very well.'

Later I came down with Pam to talk to the sheriff. Doctor Williams had been summoned to care for the hysterical Mrs. Andrews, and Phil, hearing of the disturbance, had come along to see for himself that I was unharmed.

'Chris,' he said, coming to me as I entered the parlor, 'are you all right?'

'I think so, now,' I said with a tremulous laugh. I was grateful for the concern in his eyes. I was a fool, I told myself, to moon over Gabe when someone as nice as Phil obviously cared for me.

The thought of Gabe, however, gave me a little pang of guilt, and I avoided the concern in Phil's eyes. Pam had made coffee — not very good coffee, but it was hot and strong, and I helped myself to some.

There was, after all, not much to be

told. The sheriff confirmed what Pam had already told me, that someone had fired a shotgun at the attic windows. No one had been hurt, and it looked as if the intention had been to scare those of us in the house.

'As they certainly did,' I said.

'Your sister says she found you in the hall. Can you tell me what you were doing there?'

'I couldn't' sleep. I had slept most of the afternoon and evening, so by that hour, I was wide awake. I thought I would go down to the kitchen for something to eat, and I was on my way there when the shots rang out. I'm afraid I screamed. I was badly frightened.'

Phil was sitting by me on the sofa and he reached over to clasp my hand. I saw Pam's eyebrow edge upward. I was surprised at how quickly that lie had rolled off my tongue, although I was suffering pangs of guilt because of it.

'And you heard or saw nothing that would give us a clue to who was here?'

I shook my head firmly. I had a silly fear that my voice might give me away if I spoke, but I could not give Gabe away just like that, not without giving him at least a chance to explain to me. No matter how incriminating things looked on the surface, there was still the possibility that he might have a reasonable explanation.

Reasonable to me, at any rate, but the others here would listen to it differently, because they were prejudiced against him. Not Pam, to be sure, but the sheriff, and Phil, and perhaps Doctor Williams. And Mrs. Andrews already blamed the Goins family and Gabe, and if she heard that I had seen Gabe from my window, nothing again would ever convince her that he was not trying to murder her.

The scales, in other words, were already weighted against him, and in order to make things even, I had to cheat a little. I had to tell that lie until I could see him and try to get the truth from him. After that . . . but I would cross that bridge when I came to it.

I woke to a gray day and a gloomy house. My head ached from the night's tension, and I was haunted by a sense of guilt for the lie I had told. It wasn't only Gabe's freedom at stake, nor my tender feelings. I could not help reminding myself that I was perhaps gambling with Pam's safety, and certainly with Mrs. Andrews's peace of mind. I could not indefinitely conceal Gabe's guilt, if guilt it was.

Pam's day was brightened by the news that Peter was coming home. An accidental poisoning was one thing, but murders and shootings were another, and he was plainly worried about Pam.

'I think he's being silly,' Pam said, but she looked altogether pleased by this show of concern on his part, as of course any woman would be, practical nature or no.

I still had the question of Gabe's guilt or innocence to answer, however, and I wanted to answer it as soon as possible. Shortly after lunch, I made ready for the walk to Gabe's house.

'Where are you going?' Pam asked.

'I still have Gabe Goins's jacket. I want to return it to him.'

'It seems to me that could wait,

couldn't it? After all that's gone on the last few days, I'm not sure you ought to be traipsing around in the woods by yourself.'

'I won't be by myself. I mean to take Zeke with me.'

I hurried off before she could decide that she ought to accompany me. I knew without asking what view Pam would take of my not telling what I had seen last night. She would call me a romantic fool, and probably she would be right.

But the closer Zeke and I got to the dirt road to Gabe's house, the less sure I became. What was I going to say to him? How did you ask someone if they had been guilty of crimes — not only that shooting last night, but the murder of Nellie, and all the rest, including the mysterious things that had been plaguing Mrs. Andrews? If he were innocent, he must certainly hate me for asking; and if he were guilty, I was putting a match to dynamite.

I needed to think. Leaving the path, I put Gabe's coat on the grass by a sprawling thicket of dogwood bushes and sat down on it. In the distance I could hear the creek rushing and splashing over the rocks in its bed. The pine-scented air was restful, and I leaned back.

After the hours of building tension, it was delightful just to pause here for a moment in this peaceful glade. I stared up at the sky, watching the leaves overhead quiver with each breeze. Zeke came once to look earnestly at me. Then, apparently deciding that he was not needed just now, he went off exploring on his own, leaving me alone.

I was not alone for long. I heard the sound of someone hurrying through the undergrowth. My first thought was of the danger in these hills, of someone who had cut a girl's throat and put an 'X' mark on her forehead. I half sat up, shrinking into the concealing branches of the dogwood.

In a moment, Annie, Mrs. Maywood's kitchen helper, appeared along the path, hurrying on some errand of her own. She was going in the same direction as I had been going, and traveling so quickly that, had I not left the path to rest here, she would have overtaken me.

Annie, though, was hardly a danger, and I started to get up to call after her as she went by, but before I could say her name, someone else called it.

'Annie.'

I froze where I was, neither moving nor speaking. I knew that voice; knew who had called to her even without hearing her reply.

'Gabe!' she cried, beginning to run.

Through the thick branches of the dogwood, I could see her dash into his arms — saw the two of them embrace happily, his strong brown hand stroking her bleached hair.

'Sweetheart,' I heard him call her emphatically, so that word reached me, although the rest of what they were saying was too faint for me to hear.

Sweetheart. And that embrace. Endearment. But he was not a man to throw around terms and gestures of affection. No, not he. If he called her sweetheart and embraced her and stroked her hair, he must love her, surely.

Or must pretend to.

That was unkind and yet, thinking of

him, I could not believe that he loved that poor, simple creature who was in his arms just now, the two of them talking in earnest. And if he didn't love her, then why this show of affection?

I thought of the charge Mrs. Andrews had leveled at him in regard to me — that he was using me to get close to her, to get inside the house as it were. Was he using both of us, Annie too? Was he using that pathetic girl's slow-wittedness as a means of exercising his revenge on Mrs. Andrews?

I couldn't think. I felt sick and I knew that I had somehow to get away before they saw me. I couldn't face them, not just now, not as confused as I was and as unhappy.

I pulled myself back, shrinking still further into the protective undergrowth and the weeds, until I was kneeling on the ground. I began to crawl slowly away from them. The earth sloped downward and there was a wall of bushes a few yards away. I prayed that there were no snakes between me and those bushes.

I had almost reached them when I

heard Gabe say, 'Why, it's old Zeke, from the house. What's he doing out here?'

'He didn't come with me,' Annie said.

I dived into the bushes, stretching flat on my belly, and waited. After a moment, he called my name: 'Chris. Hey, Chris, are you out there?'

I held my breath, praying that he would not come looking for me, but it occurred to me how much worse it would be if he found me like this, hiding beneath some bushes. In my agony and my desire to avoid a confrontation, I had made things far worse. Now I could only lie where I was and shiver and hope that he chose not to search for me.

For a long time there was silence. I had just decided that I was safe, and started to get to my knees again, when I saw him, standing only a few yards away. He had his head up, as if sniffing the air, and he was looking slowly from right to left. If he had dropped his eyes to the ground, he would surely have seen me.

It was Annie who saved me that humiliation. She came up behind him and tugged at his sleeve. 'There ain't nobody here. I'd have seen her if she'd been in front of me. Come on, we got to get things straightened out.'

'It's old Zeke,' he said, but he turned away from me, for which I gave silent thanks. 'He doesn't usually run loose like this.'

'Someone forgot to lock him up. Things are all in a tizzy at the house. I guess we know why, too, don't we?' She laughed, a harsh little sound, and led him away, and in a moment they were gone.

I got to my feet, crouching down, and duck-walked until I was sure I had put enough distance and trees between us. Then I stood erect and ran as best I could, finding my way eventually back to the path.

I was nearly home before Zeke caught up with me, giving me a very quizzical look as he trotted alongside me.

'Thanks for not giving me away, old friend,' I told him, and he almost seemed to nod, as if we had indeed conspired together.

Seeing him, though, reminded me of Gabe's jacket. I had left it lying on the ground back there in the woods. I dared not go back for it now, even if I were not trembling like a leaf and out of breath from running, and I could hardly think it would remain unfound by them.

Close on the heels of that thought came another — surely Gabe could not have missed seeing it. When I had seen him looking for me, he must have been standing directly over it!

16

I had been drawn still deeper into the web of fear and suspicion that held me. I could not think clearly what I should do. Reason alone told me that I should report what I knew, all of it, from the button that I had seen Gabe take from Nellie's hand, to the glimpse I'd had of Gabe crossing the lawn just before the shooting last night, and the knowledge that Gabe and Annie were, putting it in the mildest possible terms, well acquainted, sufficiently so that they had secret meetings in the woods.

The implications in this last were the most frightening. The accidents that had happened in this house that had so frightened Mrs. Andrews bespoke of someone inside the house, and now it looked as if Annie, out of blind faith, was acting as Gabe's agent here.

Every angle that I considered only made things look worse for him. Yet I still could not bring myself to make open charges against him, and it was not only my feelings for him that held me back. Strangely enough, it was Annie I was thinking of now.

She was such a pitiable creature. How easy it must have been to deceive her, to make her believe that she was loved, and how it would surely crush her to discover after all that she had only been a dupe. This was the part that hurt me the most. It was bad enough that he had deceived me, but to have been so cruel to someone as little able to look out for herself as Annie was — that was unforgivable in the man.

I rather thought they had found that coat I left behind in the woods, and guessed its significance, because when Annie served dinner that evening, I saw her give me several sidelong glances. Once our eyes met and I looked boldly back. I did not know what I meant to do, but I knew that I must soon take some course of action. However sorry I felt for her, I must remember that, if Gabe were truly guilty of the things he seemed guilty of, she was no less a victim than the rest of us were; and though she would hate me for it, I must hurt her to help her. I met her gaze, trying to show by mine that I was not timid or weak.

My suspicions were borne out when we encountered one another in the hall soon after dinner, perhaps not really by chance.

'I was wondering, miss, if you was in the woods this afternoon?' she said.

'I was,' I replied, and then, thinking it foolish to beat around the bush, I added, 'I saw you with Gabe Goins.'

She looked so very frightened that I regretted putting it so baldly. I tried to make my voice a little more kindly. 'Annie, tell me, please, are you sweethearts?'

She looked at me with those uncertain eyes of hers. I could almost hear wheels turning in her head, and I knew that she was trying to think what to say.

'Tell me one thing, then,' I said, putting a gentle hand on her arm. 'Do you love him?'

After another lengthy silence, she said, in a cautious voice, 'Yes.'

'And he says he loves you?' She nodded. 'And it is you who has caused the accidents that have happened here in the house, isn't it? The stairs, that fire, even the mushroom poisoning?'

She was not ready to go that far, however. A wary look came into her eyes and she made no reply directly to that question, but instead asked, 'You won't tell, will you, about seeing Gabe and me together?'

I bit my lip, not knowing how to answer that. I couldn't go on not telling the things I knew, but she had so frightened a look, I would have had to be far crueler than I am to say otherwise to her just then.

'Miss, don't tell, please, just for tonight,' she begged in a whisper.

'And tomorrow?'

Just at that moment, Mrs. Maywood called Annie's name from the kitchen. Annie glanced in that direction and then brought her frightened eyes back to me. 'Just don't tell for tonight.'

I sighed. 'All right. I'll make a deal. If you'll promise me no more pranks tonight, and tell Gabe I want a full explanation, I'll promise to keep your secret until tomorrow. After that, well, we'll see.'

Mrs. Maywood opened the door from the kitchen. 'There you are,' she said. 'I've got work out here for you when you've finished gabbing.'

Annie gave me a last, pleading glance and went into the kitchen, and I went along to the library to join Pam and Peter Andrews.

Peter had arrived that afternoon and Pam was behaving like any romantic, in-love young lady. Peter was pleasant and intelligent, and though not really handsome, he had an engaging, attractive manner.

The two were obviously in love, however, and had been apart for a while, and I could not help feeling my presence was an intrusion. This only made me feel all the more isolated from Pam, at the very time when I would most have liked to confide in her. I could not, of course — not on this night of all nights, and spoil Peter's homecoming for her.

'You're like a caged animal tonight,' Pam remarked once. I had, without realizing it, been pacing nervously back and forth. The temperature had dropped, and outside the windows we could see a thick fog already closing in. A fire burned in the fireplace but its cheery flames did nothing to dispel the chill I felt.

'I'm afraid I'm not very good company.'

'Poor Chris. I should have made you go to Florida after all. You still could, you know.'

But that, oddly enough, I had no desire to do. I was in it now, far enough that I wanted to see things through to whatever conclusion awaited me.

I excused myself soon after that and went up to my room. In fact, I was tired from the previous night's shattering disturbance, and I had no difficulty in getting to sleep.

I was awakened by the sound of my door opening. I thought at first it was Pam, come to look in on me, but after a few seconds someone asked in a whisper, 'Miss, are you asleep?'

'Annie,' I said, recognizing the voice. 'Come in. Turn on the light.'

She closed the door before clicking on the light. I blinked, looking at my watch. It was almost midnight. Annie was dressed in a heavy coat and a scarf, and from the moisture that glistened on them, I guessed that she had just come in from outdoors.

'What is it?'

'It's Gabe. He wants to talk to you.'

'Gabe — where is he?'

'In the woods. He told me to come and get you, and bring you to talk to him. He wants to explain everything.'

'I'll get my sister.'

'No.' Annie stepped in front of me. 'Gabe said to bring you and not to let anyone else know about it.'

I met her gaze frankly. She had a determined look, as if she had been impressed with the importance of her mission — but to go into the woods, in the middle of the night, with all that had happened already?

'He says to tell you he loves you.'

'He told you to tell me that?' She

nodded. 'But, Annie, I — I don't understand.'

'Gabe will explain everything.'

I hesitated a moment more. I could see from my window that there was a thick fog outside. Tragedy had already struck in those woods, and it could be dangerous for me to go into them alone.

No, not alone. Annie was with me, and I was going to meet Gabe. In the end, it came down to a question of whether I was really afraid of Gabe.

The answer to that was, no. Despite all the evidence against him, despite everything that I myself had seen and heard, my heart would not let me believe that Gabe was a murderer, or that I had anything to fear from him.

I dressed in a matter of minutes, donning a heavy skirt and sweater and picking a warm jacket. Annie stole from my room, turning the light off first, and looking up and down the hall, and I followed. I wore crepe-soled shoes and she had on sneakers, and we made not a sound as we crept down the stairs. In a moment we were outside.

I had an urge to change my mind when we stepped out. It was as black as pitch, and the gray fog rushed up to meet us.

The door closed with a click, and I steeled myself and asked, 'Where is he?'

'He's out in the woods. He didn't want anyone to see him.'

She started off and I followed, and in a moment the darkness and the fog had swallowed us up. I looked back, but already the house had vanished.

17

We seemed to walk for hours, but I had not brought my watch, and in that strange, unreal darkness, time was blurred. We had long since climbed the fence and entered the woods, but I was not sure where we were. I remembered the dangers here — the wild dogs in particular. By night, too, it would be incredibly easy to step into a sinkhole without warning and fall into the ground, never to escape. And somewhere here, hidden in this mist, was Devil's Pond, that deadly mudhole that waited to suck down the unwary wanderer.

I was more than a little grateful for Annie, walking just ahead of me with her flashlight, which she flicked on and off intermittently. She walked with the confident steps of one who knows her way and I watched her feet as best I could, trying to step just where she had stepped.

The fog had closed in around us with a

vengeance. I could see no more than a few feet in any direction even when the light was on. I had an eerie feeling that we were cut off on a little island of mist and wet earth, and the rest of the world about us had melted into that gray haze of nothingness.

Annie had said nothing since we left the house, except to tell me of the fence and once to warn me of a log in the path. I found my uneasiness increasing with every step. Suddenly, urgently, I wished I were back in the warmth and safety of my room.

'Is it much further?' I asked. I dared not stop, for fear she would go on and in a matter of seconds I would lose her.

'Pretty soon,' she said without slowing her pace.

'Maybe we ought to go back. The fog is awfully thick.'

'I can find my way.' She went on and I could do nothing but follow. I would never have been able to find my way back in the fog, certainly not without untold damage to my nerves at the least. I could not begin to guess at how far we had come and was not at all clear in which direction we were traveling. For all I could say, we had been walking in circles, and though we had left the house and started toward the east, we might now be west of it.

We came into a clearing. I thought it looked vaguely familiar, but in the fog that swirled ever closer and closer, the most commonplace shapes seemed changed. Even Annie, who stopped so suddenly that I almost collided with her, looked quite different. There seemed something ominous about the look she gave me. She glanced around the clearing, as if looking for something.

'Wait here.' Before I could object, she had disappeared into the darkness, leaving me alone in that little opening in the fog that seemed to grow ever denser and to advance toward me. It was eerie and unpleasant and I was sorry now that I had come at all. I stared in the direction she had gone, watching the gray swirl. It pressed closer, an airy tendril wrapping about my ankle as if to ensnare me.

I heard voices, Annie's and a man's,

and in a moment their shapes loomed up at the edge of the clearing. He was in black, so that he had the appearance of some grim phantom of the night, a shadow among shadows suddenly drifting toward me.

'Gabe,' I said, taking a step forward, but it wasn't Gabe, it was his father. The cold eyes of the elder Goins regarded me steadily as he came to where I was standing, stopping so close in front of me that I thought he was going to seize me.

'They didn't see you come out?' he asked of Annie, although his eyes never left mine.

'No, pa.' She lingered behind him.

'Where is Gabe?' I asked, trying to sound less frightened than I felt. I could not help remembering that his man had no kindliness toward me at all. His resentment of me was of the worst possible sort, because there was no reason to it. He clasped his hands over the end of the big stick he carried.

'Gabe's late. He sent me ahead to talk to you.' One corner of his mouth lifted upward in a grin, but there was nothing

242

in that expression to lift my spirits or ease my nervousness.

I looked past him at Annie, partly because I wanted to escape the chill of his gaze. 'You told me Gabe was waiting.'

He said, as if this accounted for everything, 'You wouldn't have come if she'd have told you I was waiting to see you.'

The delayed reaction went off then. It was like being hit by a ton of bricks, and I could not conceal what I was thinking. I looked from him to her and the truth jumped out at me. My mouth fell open.

'You called him pa.'

They both laughed — she soundlessly, he with a dry little chuckle that tore raggedly at my nerves.

'That's right, Annie's my little girl.'

'But . . . Mrs. Andrews doesn't know.'

'Course she doesn't. You don't think she'd have hired her if she knew, do you? Annie's got a light complexion, and she was away from here for years, up in Nashville, at a special school.'

I remembered then: Gabe had told me his sister had been away at a special school. It hadn't occurred to me what 'special school' meant, or I might have connected him with Annie right off — with Annie, his sister.

'When she came back, she had her hair peroxided, and I almost didn't know her myself, so I figured neither would old lady Andrews. I sent Annie over there, told her to say her name was Smith, and made up a story for her to tell about where she'd come from. Took her a while to learn it — she's slow — but once she's learned something, it's learned for sure. Old lady Andrews never got an idea she had one of my folks working right there in her house.'

I looked at Annie. 'Then it *was* you doing all those things to frighten her?'

'I sure scared her, didn't I?' She grinned, and I saw now that her grin was not only stupid, but wicked.

'Can't you think how cruel it's been, frightening that poor old woman?' I said, too angry to think of guarding my tongue.

'We mean to do a lot more than just frighten her afore we're done,' Goins said in a harsh voice.

'Oh, no. I'm going back there right now and tell Mrs. Andrews the truth. This business has gone quite far enough. Too far, in fact.'

I half-turned and stopped. About me, surrounding the three of us, was that swirling gray cloud. I could not even see the trees at the edge of the clearing, nor had I any notion of where I had entered the clearing. I couldn't go back. I couldn't go anywhere until one of them took me, and they knew it. They both laughed, their voices hovering eerily upon the wisps of the fog.

For a long moment, when their laughter had ended, we stood in silence, regarding one another in a measuring way. Then, unexpectedly, there was a sound in the fog — someone close, and coming closer. A twig snapped and a man swore under his breath.

They were as surprised as I. The old man moved with astonishing swiftness. In one quick move he had come to me and seized my arm in a painful grip. I was too startled to resist — doubly startled, first by the sounds of approach and then by his unexpected movement.

Another shadow loomed out of the fog and came into the clearing. He saw us and stopped. It was old man Mullins. He looked from one to the other of us. It was impossible for me to read his expression.

'Mullins,' the man holding my arm said, 'What the devil are you doing here?'

'I've been wondering the same about you,' Mullins said. 'I followed you up all the way from the fork, trying to figure what you'd be doing on the hills on a night like this, and sneaking around like you didn't want to be seen. Evening, Miss Collins.' He gave a little tip of his hat.

Goins had released my arm, but I did not try to move away. In the fog and darkness, I had no place to go.

'I want to talk to you,' Goins said. He went to Mullins and put a companionable arm about his shoulders. 'Come over here a minute.'

Mullins gave me a doubtful look, but he went along with Goins. They disappeared into the fog. I thought for a moment that Annie would go with them. She started to follow, but her father gestured with the big, knobby stick he carried, and she stayed behind with me, although she continued to stare in the direction in which the two men had disappeared.

They had not gone far, only out of our limited range of vision. I could hear their voices in a low mumble. The words were indistinguishable but the tone was argumentative. After a moment, Mullins said very loudly and very sharply, 'No! I won't stand for it!'

There were more words, the voices lifting, and suddenly a cry and the sound of a blow, a loud *crack*, as if someone had been struck by a stick. There were more oaths. There was little doubt that the two men were fighting. Annie knew it, too. She took several steps in that direction, so that she became almost invisible in the mist.

Mullins suddenly gave a loud cry, as of pain, and then he shouted, 'Run, miss, run for your life! They mean to kill you!'

As if a flash of lightning had illuminated the landscape, I saw at once that it was true. They did mean to kill me. That was why I had been brought here. Now that I knew so much — far, far, too much — I must be disposed of or their mischief halted, and neither father nor daughter had displayed any contrition.

After that shout, there was a sound of someone falling, another thud and, worst of all, silence.

18

Annie was slow, thank God for that. I lunged toward her and I caught her off balance, and gave her a shove that sent her tumbling. I didn't wait to see how she landed. Her cry was like the ringing of an alarm through the mist, but by then I was already lost in the gray swirls, stumbling blindly in what I thought was the direction we had originally come from.

I knew that Mullins was in trouble. I am no heroine and I was terrified, but I would have gone to him, and very nearly did, except that I knew my escaping would probably do more to save him than my charging to the place where he and Goins were fighting. Goins would have to let him be and come after me, and failing to find me, try to make his escape from the area, because I was sure to bring ruin down upon him now.

If, I thought grimly, I escaped. There

was little enough assurance of that. I hadn't gone more than a few feet before I nearly ran into a tree. It came out of the mist so suddenly before me that I gave a little cry, which must have been a guide for Goins. I stumbled to the side, my hands out in front of me as if I would feel my way through the fog. I made it another few yards before I brought my foot down on nothing but air, and went tumbling down a hillock to land in some brush.

I landed hard, with noise enough to attract any pursuers. Hard enough, too, to jolt me to a semblance of calm. I lay, trying to get my breath back, waiting for warning pains that would inform me of broken bones.

As I lay in that crumpled heap, I became aware of the silence. It was complete. There were no more sounds of fighting. Not even a breeze stirred the leaves. There was only the clinging dampness of the fog, and the smell of wet earth and rotting plant life, and in my mouth, the taste of fear.

I strained my eyes to see into the

darkness, listening, my nostrils flaring as if I would catch the scent of danger. The mist seemed to press down upon me, smothering me. I had no idea which way I had been running, where those fighting men had been, or where the clearing was with Annie in it.

Not, of course, that she would still be in it. She would be searching for me now, and in place of intelligence she had an animal's cunning knowledge of the woods and the fog. She knew the land — could probably traverse it blind — and the same for her father, who was certainly hunting me too.

'Chris.'

My name swept up out of the gray, like a bird taking ponderous wing. It was Gabe's voice, somewhere far off. It was impossible to tell what direction it came from, or from how far away.

'Chris? Can you hear me?'

Was he a part of it with them? I couldn't tell. What if I called to him and found my way into his arms, only to learn that he, too, meant to kill me? And even if he did not (and, please, God, I prayed, let

251

him not be a murderer), how could I say whether he was closer than his father to where I was lying, or which of them my shout would bring to me first? I was shivering, my heart crying out in reply to Gabe's call, while I bit my lips into silence.

'Miss? Are you all right?'

Another voice, closer and low. Mullins. Not dead then, but very much alive, and looking for me. Close, and just off to my left. I had only to walk, or even crawl, a few feet in that direction, until I was near enough to know that no one was between him and me, and then I could reply, speak his name softly. I raised myself on one elbow.

Something rustled beside me, and a second afterward the bush beside which I was lying moved, scraping my arm with lightly teasing fingers.

The hair stood on the back of my neck. There was no breeze. Some living thing, creeping no more than a yard away from me, had made that bush move — and the silence told me who it must be. I dared not even breathe, nor could I long hold the unnatural position in which I had frozen.

I heard him take a deep, slow breath. I prayed that the curtain of fog that hid me from him would not part. I saw a shadow move, and knew it was him, and that any movement at all on my part, even to turn the whiteness of my face away, must catch his eye and bring him to me. My fingernails dug into the heels of my hands. I felt the taste of blood in my mouth where I had bitten into my lip, trying to seal within me the scream that threatened to burst from my throat. Panic stirred within me. My entire body shook and trembled so that I feared I must start a rustling in the weeds.

He took another breath. I held mine.

'Miss? Can you hear me?' Mullins was closer, I thought. But Goins had stopped where he was. *Perhaps*, my reeling mind suggested, *perhaps he has seen me; has spotted the paleness of my skin against the dark shadows.*

'Chris!' Gabe's voice.

A chorus of sounds around me. Even the night and the woods had joined in the noisemaking. I heard the gentle drip of water from weighted leaves. There were rustlings in the grass. The blood rushing through my temples made a roar.

I closed my eyes, not wanting to see the end, not wanting to gaze upon that wicked face nor see the flash of a knife, the knife with which he must have cut Nellie's throat. The knife, surely, with which he had meant to cut mine. My arm was numb from supporting my weight. I thought at any second I must fall to the ground with a crash.

'Pa?' It was Annie, near. 'Have you found her?'

Her voice brought Mullins, who must have been coming closer. Suddenly his voice was right there, crying, 'So there ye are!' and a second later I saw his bulky form charge by within inches. He had what looked like the entire branch of a tree, swinging it from his shoulder like a club as he ran toward the father and daughter.

But they were gone, the father yelling, 'Come on, girl, git!'

The mist swallowed them up, and

Mullins after them, and I fell upon the ground, freeing my aching arm of its burden. I sobbed and tried to call out to Mullins, but nothing came out of my throat save a hoarse, croaking sound.

In the distance, fading, I heard Mullins yell, 'Goins, I'll catch ye if I've got to chase ye to hell! Ye'll pay for this wickedness.'

The panic seized me then, refusing to be put down any longer, taking me over completely. I scrambled to my feet and ran away from them, stumbling blindly through mist and darkness. I was sobbing and senseless, unable to think in any but a heedless way. I ran and cried, and the tears ran from my eyes to blend with the wet of the fog and the blood on my lips. I ran, and fell, and scrambled up to run again, and everywhere was the spider's web of gray that was drowning me.

I fell again, and it was then that reason came back to me — came back with a sound of shifting and falling earth, disappearing from beneath my hand, into the bowels of the earth.

I had brought my hand down heavily upon the thin shell of earth and twigs that covered a sinkhole. It collapsed, the dirt and debris falling into the hidden cavern beneath. A few more steps and it would have been my foot, and not my outstretched hand that went through, carrying me down into the earth. No need then for Goins and Annie to find me. Their work would be done for them, accomplished by nature.

It was the slap in the face that I needed. I had run onto Hungry Hill, with its multitude of dangerous sinkholes hidden by fallen leaves and collected debris, waiting to trap the unwary traveler. A step in any direction could send me crashing down into the earth — and somewhere here close at hand was Devil's Pond, a miniature lake of mud and ooze like quicksand, waiting to clutch my foot and slowly, inexorably, suck me under its surface to drown in mud, perhaps never to be found.

To drown or to break my neck in a fall to the bottom of an underground cavern, or to fall victim to the evil of Ned Goins, who, for all I knew, might by now have shaken off the pursuing Mullins, and circled back to find me.

I was truly amongst a multitude of devils.

19

Fear was like a crawling thing moving across my skin. I gave my head a fierce shake. Above all else, I must not succumb to panic again. I must find my way out of this treacherous region, and do so by the briefest of routes.

The fog had lifted somewhat, or else in my mad flight I had climbed above the worst of it, but its lessening did not much help. It was still night, still without moon, and I could see nothing but the shapes of a few trees, ghostlike and ominous in the darkness, and trailing still tendrils of fog like Spanish moss.

I got slowly, a bit unsteadily, to my feet, half expecting the ground beneath me to give way at any second. I turned my head from left to right. I was not even sure now in which direction I had been running when I fell. I strained every sense, trying to see or hear or even smell some clue to escape. I heard a muted sound of running water, one of the little creeks that flowed through the hills, but I had no idea which one, or where it would lead me if I were to find and follow it.

I had to do something. I could not just stand where I was, waiting for the skies to open and an angel of mercy to appear. I took a hesitant step and then another — and found my answer. The ground beneath my feet was gently sloping.

Hungry Hill was, of course, a hill. In the fog and dark, driven by panic, I must have raced up its incline without even noticing that I had left level ground — but sloping the ground was, and if I went down, I had to be taking myself off the hill and out of this minefield of holes and bogs. There were, of course, other dangers that might be waiting down there, but at this precise moment, they were less immediate.

What did frighten me was that between me and the bottom of the hill might lie another sinkhole. I had no idea how long I had been running on the hill, or how far I had penetrated into that dangerous land. I did not know where Devil's Pond

259

was. It might be just a few feet in front of me, directly in my path.

I had to will my feet to move. I stepped down upon more of the same solid earth upon which I had been standing. I tried to peer closely at the ground in front of me, but I could see nothing. I think if I could have seen, as in daylight, I would not have been so frightened; but this blackness, and the lingering swirls of fog that came and went, gave the scene a nightmare quality more horrifying than anything I had ever experienced before. Each step might be taking me to safety — or it might be taking me to my doom.

I gritted my teeth and stepped slowly forward. Fear within me kept shouting for me to run — and how desperately I wanted to obey that command — but reason held it at bay, and I went step by cautious step; and with each step, the fear lessened a little and my confidence returned, so that I had no longer to clench my fists at my sides and had begun to breathe more naturally — until I stepped into the mud.

My foot came down on water, cold and

thick, and sank down into the mud beneath it. I gasped — heaven knows how I kept from screaming my lungs out — and yanked my foot back, almost throwing myself over backward.

It was not Devil's Pond — not this time: only a little stagnant pool of water left by some now diverted or dried up run; but it had shaken my uneasy self-confidence again, and brought me once more to the verge of panic. I was shaking like a leaf, cold, and not only from the water. I felt out with my foot, feeling my way around the edge of that little puddle, not wanting another soaking.

It was behind me, finally. I looked down, seeing so faintly a reflection upon its surface. I started off again, and froze at a black shape before me.

It was only a tree, however — half-fallen, with branches draped upon the ground. It gave me encouragement. Surely a tree that substantial couldn't have been growing right in Devil's Pond. It had to signify solid ground.

I went cautiously toward it, reaching

out before myself like a blind woman. I caught hold of a slender finger of a branch, and even that gave me courage. In a moment, I was leaning against the trunk, half-sitting on one of the down-slanting branches. I needed to rest for a moment, to get my breath and re-steady my nerves.

I had been breaking the stillness of the night with my progress down the hillside, my feet stirring long-since fallen leaves and twigs, my skirt making little rustling sounds where it brushed the growth. I stood for perhaps a full moment at the downed tree before something came through the mists, hampering my thinking — the sounds were continuing. I was standing motionless, but there were still footsteps moving through leaves and twigs, still rustlings from the brush.

I had been so absorbed in picking my way step by step through the dangers of this hill, that I had forgotten that two, maybe three, people were out there in that darkness looking for me to murder me — and there, surely, was one of them, close on my trail.

I crawled over the branch I had been leaning on and dropped to the ground behind it. There was some undergrowth there, too: weeds and brush that hid me like a blanket. By now I was numb, too battered by fear even to tremble. I could only crouch and wait, and one part of my brain began to pray.

'Chris?'

It was a tiny whisper, so soft that it might have been a breeze sighing through the trees.

'Chris?'

Closer now, but still soft, like mist calling me. The devils said to haunt the hills, the devils who danced on the grass, calling me to dance with them, inviting me to my death. My mind was so buffeted by fear and exhaustion that I thought I heard the piping of their horns, and crouched as I was in the grass, my feet stirred. At any moment I expected to see the ring of shadowy figures, see one of them turn and spy me, and beckon me to join them, and I would rise and go and dance, and the nightmare would be ended at last.

'Chris, where are you?'

It was Gabe's voice. Gabe, slipping through darkness and mist, groping his way as I had done, calling my name. To save me, or to slay me? God help me, I didn't know which. I couldn't reason now; my brain was tortured beyond rational thinking. He was one of them, wasn't he? I had seen him myself at the house before that shooting incident, and even if until now he had been somehow innocent, it was his father and his sister who were involved in murder. He had to think of them — had to help them, didn't he? It would be asking a great deal of him to expect him to protect me at their expense.

I wanted to call to him, to stand and run into his arms. Lord, Lord, how I wanted to do that, but I couldn't. It wasn't only my life in the balance now. So long as I remained free, Mullins was safe. They could hardly murder him with me to witness against them — but if I were dead, then he was the only witness left, and his life was worth nothing.

The tears came to my eyes and I

pressed myself flat against the ground and cried, muffling my sobs with my hand, but I couldn't risk turning to Gabe now. I had to assume that he was one of them until somewhere out of this crazy, fear-driven night, I could find the truth among all the confusing wisps of half-truth and myth and outright lies.

He was gone. I heard him still calling my name, the whispers fading on the wind, and heard his footsteps drifting further and further away. And at last the mist was silent, and I was alone once more.

I got to my feet again. I felt incredibly old and weary, beaten down by the decision I'd had to make. I could no longer feel even the icy fear that had pursued me through this night. I started out down the hill again, plodding, hardly bothering to watch where I was going. I kept my eyes down on the ground where I stepped, but that was all. I had virtually forgotten the pits, the mud hole, the others in the night. I was remembering that plaintive whispering of my name, fading into the distance.

Thinking unhappily of Gabe, I walked into his father's arms.

Into his arms, literally. I had come to a path and had begun to follow it down the hill, thinking that now the worst of it was over. It led me on a sloping course about a patch of thick brush and trees and rocks, a blind curve. I came around it and collided with the elder Goins, hurrying toward me.

Instinct alone came to my rescue. A little bubble of a scream rose in my throat and sputtered out — but he was as startled as I. Perhaps he, too, had been thinking of the demons that roamed these hills at night. He jumped back, off balance, and in one mad instantaneous dash I was off the path and racing into the darkness, back up the hill, scrambling over rocks and through berry bushes whose thorns tore at me. I leapt a shimmering stream, and half-crawled, half-flew up a crest of land that made a little bluff over the stream.

'Stop,' he shouted, and his voice was like a shot of adrenalin that sent me in a mighty exertion over that hillock to my feet again, and running, running. I ran, and hardly knew that the ground had gone soft beneath me. I brought my feet up and down, up and down, and up and down again, before it finally came through my terror-wracked brain that they were lifting off the ground not at all, but the ground was holding to them, giving a little before sucking them back down, and though I was still going through the faltering motions of running, I wasn't going anywhere. I was only standing in the same place, sloshing my feet about in the mud.

Not, though, ordinary mud, that slipped and slimed and fell away from your feet. This was something alive and clinging, something that seized me and held me and drew me into a sucking embrace. It was like one of those crawling horrible monsters from the pit, pulling you inescapably into itself.

Devil's Pond! I had run right into it, plunged into its very center before I realized where I was, and it had me now. It held me fast!

20

In a moment there was the sound of someone running, and a flashlight beam shone in my face.

'Help me!' I cried, struggling without success to free my feet from the sucking mud that held me fast now. It was already up to my ankles.

The light went out, and Ned Goins said, 'It's just as well this way.'

'You can't let me die here,' I sobbed. He laughed, and that rasping sound sobered me a little. He could, of course, just let me die where I was. Death was nothing new to him.

In a moment Annie appeared behind him. The mist was nearly gone now, and my eyes had grown accustomed to the darkness, enough for me to make out their faces and see the horrible expectant expression upon them.

'You killed Nellie. The two of you. But

why? She wasn't an Andrews, and neither am I.'

I saw him nod his head. 'Yeah, I meant to get old lady Andrews. I still will, but I wanted to scare her half to death first. But Nellie saw Annie and me together one day. I knew it wouldn't take her long to put things together in her head, and figure out who Annie was. Then she'd have told Andrews, and Annie'd have been fired, and we'd have been right back where we started, and she'd have gone right on being Miss Fat Cat.' He spat out of the corner of his mouth. 'So Annie went over there and told Nellie she had to show her something, something secret, and that fool girl come out with her to where I was waiting.'

The mud was drawing me down. I was in above my ankles now, and my mind was whirling. Panic fluttered its wings like a black bird inside my head, but I fought it back. I had to think, think of some way to free myself. I thought of Mullins. He might still be near, but if I screamed, Goins might push me under the mud. I could only wait and pray that the sound of our voices might attract him, or even Gabe.

'Gabe wasn't a part of it, was he?' I asked. I willed myself not to struggle. I had a vague memory of something I had heard or read, that struggling made you sink faster. It was the worst sort of torture, standing trapped in that ooze, terror like the ringing of a knell within me, and making myself stand still.

He laughed again. 'Nope. I had his coat on the day we got Nellie. I thought if she got a glimpse of me waiting, she'd think it was him and not be so nervous. People never minded him as much. I expect it was because of his citified ways.'

'No, it's because they feel he's not as consumed by hate as you. Can't you see what you're doing to yourself and to Annie? It isn't only you who will go to prison, it's your daughter as well.'

'Nothing'll happen to Annie. Prison? Ha! You're the only one who knows who she is, and you ain't ever going to be able to tell anybody, are you, now?'

He poked at me with his stick, as if he

meant to push me beneath the surface of the mud. He had little need to do so. My legs were trapped now, nearly to the knees, and I felt as if I were sinking faster and faster.

'For the love of heaven, help me out of here!'

'I can't do that. You'd go tell Andrews, and the next thing you know I'd be in jail, and they'd be putting rope around my neck.'

I screamed then. I couldn't help it. I was too terrified to remain calm any longer. I was being drawn down to death, to an eternity encased in this horrible mud.

'Shut up! Shut up, or I'll . . . '

I was crying now, sobbing helplessly. I was doomed. Nothing short of a miracle could save me now.

But I got my miracle, in the form of that divine messenger, Gabriel. There was a crackling of twigs and branches and a moment later Gabe appeared. His glance took in everything at once, and he began to remove his jacket.

'Hang on, Chris, I'll have you out of

there in a minute.'

'Son,' Ned Goins said, laying a hand on Gabe's arm, 'let her go.'

My heart stopped beating. Could Gabe refuse his own father's plea?

'That's the woman I love in there,' Gabe said, shaking off the restraining hand.

'If you pull her out, she'll hang me. You want to see that happen? Your own pa!'

Gabe yanked his jacket off. His father suddenly struck out with the stick in his hand. Gabe saw it coming and dodged the blow, so that it only grazed his shoulder. In a second, the two were locked in combat.

It was a nightmare, trapped in that mud, feeling it creeping ever higher and higher, while those two fought for my life no more than yards from me. It seemed to last an eternity, although in reality it could not have been more than a few seconds before Gabe struck his father a blow on the chin that knocked the older man cold.

There were no seconds to spare, now. He let his father sink to the ground, and even as he was throwing the end of his jacket to me, he said to Annie, 'Go down to the Andrews house and tell them to get the sheriff here quick.'

She hesitated, looking in confusion from him to the unconscious figure of her father, but she was accustomed to being told what to do, and when he said sharply, 'Do as I say, right now!' she took off at a run for the house.

On first try the jacket went too far to the left for me to reach it, but on the second I caught the sleeve.

'Hold tight,' he said, bracing his feet and beginning to pull me from the grip of the slime.

How can I describe the tug of war between good and evil, between life and death? I was terrified that at any moment the jacket would tear, the threads holding it together would fail, and I would plunge once again into Devil's Pond.

But it held, and Gabe, as I should have known, was stronger than any devil. I held to the cloth till my arms were numb, and he dragged me over the surface of the pond to the bank.

Finally I was in his arms, and he was kissing away my tears, and all of the devils had been defeated.

*   *   *

Those hills might be haunted by devils, but on that night I had been protected by angels. Mullins, as he explained later, had suspected from the time of Nellie's death who was responsible for it. Only one Melungeon man hated that violently. He had been keeping an eye ever since on Ned Goins, and on that night had seen Ned stealing off into the woods to meet me.

As for Gabe, he had only recently returned to the area, and had not even known where it was that Annie was working, but the finding of his missing button in Nellie's lifeless hand had told him that his father must be involved. When he learned that Annie was working at the Andrews house, he had met with her in the woods to pry the truth from her.

'I should have gone to the sheriff right

then,' Gabe said when he told me about it.

'You can't be blamed for hesitating. That's not an easy decision to make. I thought you were somehow to blame, and I put off doing anything about that.'

He smiled at me and squeezed my hand. 'I'd been out tonight — nowhere in particular, just walking around trying to think — but I knew no matter how I rationalized it, he must have committed murder. I came home and went straight to his room. I meant to make him give himself up. When I found he wasn't there, I made my mother tell me where he had gone. That's when I came out into the woods, looking for you. When I heard all the commotion, I knew what was happening.'

'I heard you calling my name, but I was so afraid. I thought surely you couldn't turn against your own father.'

'That took a great deal of character,' Mrs. Andrews said.

Miraculously, we were all seated in her parlor: she in a robe, still wearing a snood over her hair; Pam nestled sleepily in

Peter's arms. The sheriff had taken Ned Goins and Annie away, after promising that his wife would take charge of Annie and see that she was well cared for.

'Thank you, ma'am,' Gabe said to Mrs. Andrews.

That was not the least surprising event of the night. At first, Mrs. Andrews had made her predictable objections to having Gabe there; but since he was carrying me, still coated in mud and slime, in his arms, she could hardly refuse to let him come in. And when she heard even part of what had happened, she relented — with, of course, no little insistence on the part of Pam and Peter. And, I suspect, her curiosity played a part too. This was going to be a story to tell for many years. Maybe her best story.

She and Gabe regarded one another for a moment. Then he stood and stretched. It was nearly dawn. 'Guess I'd better think of going home,' he said. A note of sadness crept into his voice. I thought what a sad place home must be for him this morning. 'I appreciate your letting me come in like this,' he said to Mrs. Andrews.

'You must come again,' she said sincerely. There was no booming welcome, no flinging wide of arms. The past did not die that easily, but I felt that there was a start between them, a beginning of mutual respect that must eventually put that old demon, prejudice, to rest. In any case, she knew now who it was that had been haunting her, and it had not been demons, and it had not been Gabe, either.

He looked around the room at the rich furnishings and the elaborate moldings and heavy draperies. 'You know,' he said, 'all these years I've envied and hated you because of this place, thinking it ought to be in my family. I never really wanted it for myself. It's not my kind of place, but I thought it ought to be in my family.' He paused and thought for a moment. 'Well, I guess in a sense it will be now, won't it?

Mrs. Andrews's eyes narrowed. 'How do you mean?' she asked suspiciously. Old prejudices do not die in an instant.

'Pam's going to marry your son, isn't

she? And she's Chris's sister. That'll make her my sister-in-law. That's family, isn't it?'

Mrs. Andrews shook her head. 'No, only if you were to marry . . . oh.' She looked at me, and then back to him, and a smile broke upon her face. 'I see,' she said.

And, at last, so did I.

THE END

Other titles in the
Linford Mystery Library:

ROSE POINT

V. J. Banis

Karen marries Alan Denver and returns with him to the cliff-side house next to the lighthouse he tends. However, she knows nothing of the death — or even the existence — of his first wife. Then she begins to sense strange ghostly presences about the house, and her husband starts behaving oddly. She senses, too, that Alan's mother, who lives nearby, is trying to break up her marriage — but why? The truth lies hidden behind a locked door, and in a scrap of rose point lace . . .

THE CORPSE IN CACTUS

Lonni Lees

The murder that Detective Maggie Reardon has solved at a local Tucson art gallery creates unforeseen difficulties in her personal life. Then, to complicate matters, a corpse is discovered at a museum lying under a bed of cactus. What at first appears to be a tragic accident quickly starts to smell like murder. Maggie's been dealt a nameless victim with no witnesses, no suspect, and no apparent cause of death. And as the evidence unfolds, she must also battle a hostile fellow cop, determined to see her lose her badge . . .

MISSION OF MERCY

John Robb

A revolution breaks out in the independent Arab republic of Hanah. The French legation is in danger. A tiny Foreign Legion detachment is sent into the country, ordered to protect European lives and property. But that detachment is in no condition to undertake a task that calls for restraint as well as courage. It is under the command of Captain Laubert, a cunning but demented officer . . . a man who has been threatened with arrest by his junior officer.